'I don't suppose you'd like to do that again?'

'This?' She kissed Tom's cheek again.

'Yeah.' He didn't move his hands from the countertop, but dipped his head to touch his lips to her forehead. All Cori could think about was making this real. Letting go of the pretence and doing the one thing she wanted to do. She slid her hand over the soft wool of his sweater, up to the collar of his shirt. At the first touch of her fingers on his skin she heard his uneven intake of breath.

When she curled her arm around his neck, pulling him down towards her, he drew her in close, making sure that she felt his body against hers before she had a chance to feel his lips. He wanted her. The knowledge spilled into her like bright light penetrating a very dark place. *He wanted her.*

Dear Reader,

For me, writing isn't just a job—it's a lifeline. When something's bothering me I write it down. When I'm happy about something I write it down. For as long as I can remember the page has been my faithful confidante.

So I can understand how Cori Evans operates. As an art therapist she is used to helping children express themselves through the medium of art, and her painting expresses her own thoughts and feelings as well. But Tom Riley's burden of secrets is her greatest challenge yet.

I hope you enjoy this book—it's one I've long wanted to write. I always enjoy hearing from readers, and you can contact me via annieclaydon.com.

Annie x

DISCOVERING DR RILEY

BY
ANNIE CLAYDON

This is a work of fiction. Names, characters, places, locations and incidents are purely fictional and bear no relationship to any real life individuals, living or dead, or to any actual places, business establishments, locations, events or incidents. Any resemblance is entirely coincidental.

First published in Great Britain 2016
By Mills & Boon, an imprint of HarperCollins*Publishers*
1 London Bridge Street, London, SE1 9GF

© 2016 Annie Claydon

ISBN: 978-0-263-26369-5

Our policy is to use papers that are natural, renewable and recyclable products and made from wood grown in sustainable forests. The logging and manufacturing processes conform to the legal environmental regulations of the country of origin.

Printed and bound in Great Britain
by CPI Antony Rowe, Chippenham, Wiltshire

Cursed with a poor sense of direction and a propensity to read, **Annie Claydon** spent much of her childhood lost in books. A degree in English Literature followed by a career in computing didn't lead directly to her perfect job—writing romance for Mills & Boon—but she has no regrets in taking the scenic route. She lives in London: a city where getting lost can be a joy.

Books by Annie Claydon

Mills & Boon Medical Romance

All She Wants For Christmas
Doctor on Her Doorstep
The Doctor Meets Her Match
The Rebel and Miss Jones
Re-awakening His Shy Nurse
Once Upon a Christmas Night...
200 Harley Street: The Enigmatic Surgeon
A Doctor to Heal Her Heart
Snowbound with the Surgeon
Daring to Date Her Ex
The Doctor She'd Never Forget

Visit the Author Profile page at millsandboon.co.uk for more titles.

To Lynn
With thanks for helping me count the days

Praise for
Annie Claydon

CHAPTER ONE

'DO ME A FAVOUR…'

There was more than a hint of flirtatiousness about the tone of the request, but Tom Riley knew that Dr Helen Kowalski's designs on his person were far from recreational. A Sunday afternoon, a doctor at a loose end and a phone call from a busy A and E department added up to only one thing.

'You want me to come down and see someone?'

'If you're not busy on the ward. We've got a kid here who's driving everyone crazy.'

'And since he's under sixteen, you thought you might pass him on to me.' Tom smirked into the phone. 'Because awkward customers are my speciality.'

Helen snorted with laughter. 'I could say something about it taking one to know how to deal with one.'

'If you do, I'm going home. I'm not even supposed to be at work today.'

'Get down here, Tom.' A crash sounded from somewhere in the background and Helen muttered a curse. 'Please…'

'I'm already on my way.'

The source of all the trouble turned out to be eight years old, with a shock of red hair. He was sitting on the bed

in one of the cubicles, swinging his legs. Tom gave him a
wide berth to avoid being kicked, and smiled at the woman
sitting next to him.

'I'm Dr Tom…' He winced, stepping back as he realised
that he'd underestimated the reach of the boy's flailing feet.

'I'm so sorry… Adrian, please don't do that, you'll hurt
someone.' It looked as if Adrian's companion had come
straight from some half-completed DIY project, with her
dark hair fastened at the back of her head and bound with
a scarf. Paint-stained overalls had been slipped from her
shoulders, with the sleeves tied around her waist, to reveal
a Fair Isle sweater with a darn at one elbow.

'No harm done.' Tom dismissed the urge to rub his leg
where Adrian had kicked him. 'What brings you here?'

When she looked up at him, it registered that she had
violet eyes. Whatever *had* brought her here seemed suddenly unimportant.

'It's Adrian.' She turned wearily to the boy, laying her
free hand on one flailing leg in an attempt to restrain him.
Tom noticed that the other was held fast in Adrian's own
hand. 'He's hit his head. There's a lump.'

'Okay.' Tom wondered whether Adrian was usually
this badly behaved. 'Anything else? Any change in his
demeanour?'

Her wry smile was directed at the boy, who promptly
stopped kicking his feet. 'He always has plenty of energy.'

That was one way of putting it. 'So what happened?'

'I was up a ladder and Adrian was playing. He brushed
against the ladder and we both ended up on the floor. He
banged his head, so I thought it was best to bring him here
and get him checked over.'

She tipped her face back towards Tom, raking him with
her gaze. He could almost feel it caress his face, before
she looked away.

'You weren't hurt?' Instinct told him that Adrian had probably careened straight into the ladder, rather than merely brushing against it. And the stiff way that she moved told him that Adrian wasn't the only one who should see a doctor.

'I'm fine.' She couldn't even meet his querying look. 'Adrian, don't do that, please.'

Tom focussed his attention back on the boy and saw that he had started to meticulously shred the paper cover that had been laid over the top of the bed. First things first. 'Right, young man. Let's take a look at that head of yours.'

Adrian's freckled face and red hair seemed to flame. He clutched fiercely at the woman, and she winced. Tom backed off. Experience had told him that it was always good to listen to adults, but that you learnt a great deal more by looking at a child.

Pulling a chair away from the bed a little, he sat down, leaning back and folding his arms. Now that there was no imminent danger of being wrestled from the grip of his companion, Adrian calmed, regarding him steadily.

'All right, Adrian.' Tom stretched his legs out in front of him, as if he had all the time in the world. 'How are we going to do this?'

This doctor was a dream. Cori had known that taking Adrian to A and E was going to be a challenge, but he needed to be examined by a doctor, and on a Sunday afternoon there wasn't a great deal of choice but to join the queue and try to reassure him and keep him calm. The loud farting noises that he had made in the waiting room had ensured a circle of empty chairs around them, and the woman doctor that Adrian had seen at first had been kind and efficient but clearly too busy to give him the time he needed.

She hadn't caught this doctor's second name, and perhaps he hadn't given it. He wasn't wearing a name badge like the other staff in A and E, but more importantly he'd had the time and the inclination to sit back and let Adrian dictate the pace. He'd explained everything that he was about to do, and nodded when Cori had added the piece of information that she knew Adrian needed to hear. He'd be going home with her, as soon as they were finished here.

The man was blond and blue-eyed, but gifted with enough hard edges to indicate that he was probably no angel. He hadn't tried to part her and Adrian either, but had somehow contrived to examine Adrian while he'd still clung to her. When his fingers had accidentally brushed her cheek, she'd forgotten the pain in her hip and shoulder and had felt herself automatically relax.

'Right, then, Adrian.' Tom grinned. 'I'm officially giving you a clean bill of health. That means you can go home with your...' His gaze flipped questioningly towards Cori.

'Sister.' She volunteered the closest description she could manage without a lengthy explanation.

He nodded gravely, clearly taking a shot at estimating the eighteen-year difference between Adrian's age and hers. 'Right. Your sister.'

Perhaps he'd come to the conclusion that they came from a large family, which was close enough to the truth. Cori nudged Adrian, who was now beaming at Tom.

'Thank you,' Adrian responded to her prompt, and Tom smiled again. He had a nice smile, which came packaged up with a small nod, as if he was sharing a secret. Cori reminded herself that, whatever the conspiracy was, it was probably between him and Adrian and not her.

'You're very welcome. You were right to come.' He turned his attention to Cori, and she felt her fingertips tingle. That was probably the effect of having fallen hard on her left side, although why her right hand should be affected as well was beyond her.

'How are you getting home?'

'My father's coming to pick us up. He should be here by now.'

'All right. What's his name?'

'Ralph Evans. But—'

'Stay there.' Tom's look brooked no argument. 'I'll see if I can find him.'

Adrian was clearly still determined not to be parted from his sister, and so Tom was going to have to find a way of examining her without distressing the boy. Because however much Adrian wanted to go home, and however much his sister tried to hide it, she was clearly in pain. And as much as he prided himself on his medical skills, Tom was unable to tell whether her ribs were broken by simply looking at her.

He caught Helen's eye as she hurried past. 'Have you got a minute? I want you to have a look at the woman that the boy came in with.'

'What's the matter with her?'

'She's had a fall. If you could just check her over...'

Helen shook her head. 'If she's not urgent then she'll have to wait. The boy's father was here a minute ago.'

'You get on. I'll find him.'

Helen shot him a smile over her shoulder, and Tom looked around the busy department for some clue as to who the father might be. Maybe red hair, which matched the boy's...

A middle-aged man turned towards him, following the receptionist's pointing finger. 'Dr Riley? I'm here for Adrian Harper, I'm his guardian.'

Tom's surprise must have shown on his face. In his experience you could often explain a child's behaviour when you met the parent, but this man, with his relaxed manner and dark, salt-and-pepper hair, bore no resemblance to Adrian at all. Before he could frame the question, the man had reached into his pocket and drawn a card from his wallet to identify himself.

'Adrian's your foster son?'

Ralph nodded. 'Is he all right?'

'He has a bit of a bump on his head.' Tom remembered the pamphlets on aftercare that were stacked behind Reception and reached across, selecting the right one and handing it to Ralph. 'You should keep an eye on him for the next twenty-four hours.'

Ralph chuckled. 'We always do. Is Cori all right?'

'His sister?' Tom realised that he didn't know her name. Her smile and the extraordinary colour and warmth of her eyes had seemed enough.

'Yes. When she called she said that Adrian had cannoned into a ladder. I was rather hoping she hadn't been up it at the time.'

Cori had obviously rationed out the truth, giving little bits of it as and when she'd reckoned necessary. 'She told me he brushed against the ladder and that she'd fallen. I'd like her to see a doctor, as she's obviously in pain, but Adrian won't let go of her.'

Ralph nodded, clearly not fazed by any of this. 'Okay, thanks. I'll take Adrian home and make sure that Cori sees someone.'

'Today.' Tom peered through to the waiting room, which, if anything, looked even fuller than it had been half an hour ago. 'If she comes back here, I'll try and find someone who'll see her quickly.'

'Thanks. I know how busy you are, and I appreciate it. She'll be back as soon as I've got Adrian into the car.'

* * *

Cori walked back from the hospital car park. Adrian had been mollified by her assertion that she wasn't coming with them because she was going straight back to her own flat, but Ralph had insisted quietly that she do nothing of the sort. Now she had at least another two-hour wait in front of her before she saw one of the doctors in A and E.

The pain in her shoulder and hip was getting worse, though, and now that she was alone Cori suddenly wanted to cry. She couldn't be injured, not now. Tomorrow morning she'd be starting an eight-week attachment, here at the hospital, which might lead to getting the permanent post that she really wanted. However hard she'd fallen, she couldn't afford not to get up and get on with it.

'Hey, there.'

That sounded suspiciously like Tom's voice, laced with a hint of the conspiratorial quality of his smile. She looked up, and saw him standing outside the entrance to the A and E department, a cup of coffee in his hand. He looked like a dream come true.

'Come along.' He took a long swig of the last of his coffee and spun the paper cup into the bin.

She wanted to just go with him, without asking where or why. But that wasn't going to get her out of there any quicker. 'I've got to go and register at Reception. Get my place in the queue.'

He grinned and Cori hesitated. When he smiled, he was the most perfect man that she had ever seen. Wherever it was that he wanted her to go, it suddenly seemed like a good idea.

'You've just jumped the queue.'

'But…' It was tempting. 'There are people waiting. You should see them first.'

'I'm off shift, and there's nothing more for me to do here. And you've already waited once.'

Did he have to be quite so persuasive? 'It's okay, really. I appreciate it, but you should go home if your shift has finished.'

His brow darkened. '*You're* not going to kick me, are you?'

She shook her head, silently.

'Good. In that case, you'd better follow me.' He turned on his heel, not waiting for the objection that Cori felt duty-bound to make, and led the way back into A and E.

Tom hadn't given her the chance to protest any further. He'd taken one look at the rapidly forming bruises on Cori's shoulder and hip, and filled out a form for her to take down to X-Ray. While he was waiting for her, Helen had made the most of the opportunity and passed a couple of minor cases to him, telling him that she couldn't bear the thought of seeing him bored.

When they came through, he reviewed the X-rays carefully, and then went to find Cori. She was sitting on a chair in one of the cubicles, a hospital gown pulled down over her knees, her T-shirt and sweater wrapped in a bundle and hugged against her chest.

'I wanted to say thank-you, for being so nice with Adrian. And that I'm sorry he kicked you. I hope he didn't hurt you too much.' She blurted the words out almost as soon as he drew the curtain across the entrance to the cubicle.

'It's okay. I've had worse.' A lot worse. He'd grown up with it, and Tom had learned to just take the blows and move on. To cry later, when he was alone in his bed. He pushed the memory away, wondering why it had chosen that moment to surface. Maybe it had been something to do with the gentle way that Cori had treated Adrian. Tenderness always seemed to awaken an obscure feeling of loss in him.

'So what were you painting?' He didn't want to think about it any more, and Cori seemed nervous. Small talk would hopefully rectify both those issues.

'It was a wall.' She seemed to relax a bit. 'Actually, a mural. In my spare time I work with a group of artists, which donates wall art to charities and schools.'

'Sounds great. Only Adrian had different ideas?'

She stiffened. 'He didn't mean to do it. He's not usually as naughty as when you saw him...'

He liked the way she rose to the boy's defence, her eyes flashing defiance at him. 'That's okay. I'm not blaming him for anything.'

'No. Thank you. Adrian hasn't had things very easy in the last few years.'

'Your father told me he's fostered with your family.'

'Yes, that's right. He's had a few really bad experiences with hospitals.' She clutched at her sweater, as if she felt she'd just made a *faux pas*. 'Not this one.'

'No hospital's an easy place to be for a child. We do our best, but...'

'I know. You were great with him, and I really appreciate it. It makes a difference.' She seemed unwilling to let the point go. 'When he was little, he was taken into his local A and E department with his mother. Drugs overdose. The boyfriend forgot all about Adrian and he got left in the waiting room on his own. The staff found him curled up in a corner.'

A little boy, lost and alone. Tom felt a sudden heaviness in his chest, as if something was trying to stop him from breathing. 'Which is why he wouldn't let go of you?'

'Yes. And why I said there was nothing wrong with

me.' She shrugged, and winced painfully. 'I shouldn't be telling you all this, but I guess it's okay, since you're his doctor. And I wanted you to know how much the way you treated him will have meant to him. He doesn't have the words to say it. Not yet anyway.'

For a moment, Tom really couldn't breathe, and felt himself begin to choke. Then self-control came to his rescue. 'Thanks for telling me. Adrian's lucky to have you to speak up for him.'

'I'm adopted too.' She gave him a bright smile. 'I was lucky to have someone speak up for me when I needed it.'

And now she was paying it forward. Tom turned quickly, trying to shut out the *what if*s. The fact was that no one had spoken up for him when he'd been a child, and it was far too late for anyone to do it now. He moved the bed down so she could sit on it without him having to help her up, and motioned her towards it.

'Your X-rays are fine, so there are no breaks or fractures, but I'd like to check on the movement in your shoulder.'

She nodded, rising stiffly from the chair and sitting down on the bed. Tom raised it until they were almost face to face, trying not to allow her eyes to distract him from the job in hand.

'I'm going to rotate your shoulder. It's going hurt a little bit but try and relax.'

She smiled again, almost as if she was trying to reassure him. But he wasn't supposed to be noticing her smile, let alone allowing himself to react to it like a teenager. 'It already hurts a little bit.'

'Right. Then it's going to hurt a little bit more.'

It hurt. He was gentle, and measured, but it still hurt.

'Sorry... Nearly done.'

She let out the breath she'd been holding. Somehow she'd let go of the edge of the bed, and her fingers had clutched at the closest thing to hand, the material of his white coat. She felt herself flush, and let go, hoping he hadn't noticed.

'Everything's fine there. I just want to take another look at the bruising. If you could slip the gown off your shoulder...'

Cori did as he asked with trembling fingers. It was nothing. She'd shown her shoulders in public before without a second thought. But even though Tom had his back turned and was scribbling something on her notes, she was suddenly embarrassed. In the moment before she'd let go of his coat, she'd felt hard muscle flexing beneath her hand.

He was cool, and professional, his gloved fingers gently probing her shoulders and back. That just made things worse. If he'd cracked a joke, at least she could have come back with a smart reply to take the edge off the tension. Cori squeezed her eyes closed, dropping her head forward.

'Okay. That's good.' He didn't seem aware of the fact that her forehead was resting against his shoulder, and that they were in an awkward replica of an embrace. When he stepped away again, she wanted to pull him back.

'You can get dressed now.' His cool professionalism told Cori that the closeness was all in her head. She was just another patient in a never-ending line of them, and he'd been nice to her because he was probably nice to everyone.

'Thanks. I appreciate everything you've done.' She waited for him to lower the level of the bed so she could slip off it easily.

'All part of the service. I'll write a prescription for some painkillers, and see if I can find a leaflet for you to take away.' A hint of humour shone in his eyes. 'Apparently we have a leaflet for pretty much everything.'

He turned his back and then he was gone, leaving Cori to pull her T-shirt and sweater back on as quickly as her shaking, painful limbs would allow.

When she'd let out that choking gasp of pain, and reached for him, Tom had almost forgotten what he was supposed to be doing and given her a hug to comfort her. Then he'd reminded himself where he was, and had drawn back. He gave her more than enough time to get changed, and headed back to the cubicle, finding her dressed and ready to go.

He handed her the leaflet and she took it, scanning the page. 'This tells you what you can do to make yourself more comfortable. You should take it easy for a few days. You have some deep bruising and it'll hurt in the morning.'

She twisted her mouth downwards in an expression of dismay. 'I start a new job tomorrow. Here, actually.'

'You'd be better off staying at home.' Then the words sank in. 'Here?'

'Yes, I'm an art therapist. I'm here for eight weeks, starting tomorrow...'

Cori? Corrine Evans? Suddenly Tom's mouth went dry. *This* was the woman that he'd tried to keep out of his department?

'It's going to be quite a challenge and I can't take time off...' She looked at him earnestly.

He was the challenge she was talking about. And the determined look on her face told him exactly what she meant to do with that challenge.

'I'm sure...'

What was he sure of? That he happened to know that Dr Thomas Riley, Acting Head of Paediatrics, would be more than happy to give her the next two days off? That he'd actually be more than happy to give her the whole of the next eight weeks off?

Before he could come to a decision on how to break the news, she stood up. 'I won't take up any more of your time. Thank you. I really appreciate all you've done.' She shot him a bright smile, thanked him and then she was gone.

Corrine Evans. Even her name seemed to have gained an allure now that he had met her. He'd expected that he would be able to largely ignore the new art therapist, sideline her by giving her a few things to do that couldn't cause any trouble, and get on with his own job of running the department. In eight weeks' time she'd be gone and out of his hair.

Something deep in the pit of his stomach told him that it wasn't going to be that easy.

CHAPTER TWO

CORI WOKE FEELING as if she'd been run over by a steam-roller in the night. Perhaps she'd feel better once she'd had a shower and got moving.

There wasn't much choice in the matter. Her supervisor had told her that Dr Shah, Head of Paediatrics, had taken extended medical leave, and that the acting head had expressed concern about her being allowed to work in the unit. She wasn't going to give him any excuses to dismiss her before she'd even had a chance to show what she could do. Not turning up on the first day would be like presenting him with her head on a plate.

She'd packed everything she'd thought she might need for the day in a large canvas bag, which sat in the hall. Taking the heaviest and least essential items back out, she pulled the strap across her shoulder, decided she could manage, and called a taxi.

The two miles to the hospital was easy, but by the time she'd found her way through the maze of corridors to the paediatric unit her shoulder was on fire and she needed to sit down. The entrance doors to the unit were locked, and pressing the bell didn't elicit an immediate response.

'I thought I told you to stay home for a couple of days.' The voice behind her was unmistakable. Dammit. What was *he* doing here? A and E was on the other side of the building.

It was just as well that Cori could only turn slowly as it gave her time to think. 'Actually, you told me to take it easy for a couple of days.'

He didn't look best pleased. 'So I did. And I can see that you're following my instructions to the letter.' He reached past her and punched a code into the pad by the door, then held it open for her. Dressed in a suit, instead of the dark blue chinos he'd been wearing yesterday, he seemed a lot less approachable, if no less handsome.

'Thanks. I'm looking for the admin office…' Hopefully Tom wasn't going to be staying around long enough to mention that she'd turned up to work against doctor's orders. That wasn't the start she'd been hoping to make.

'I'm Tom Riley.' He pulled the door closed behind them. 'Acting Head of Paediatrics.'

Suddenly Cori's shoulder stopped hurting, in response to an instinctive urge to either fight or fly. The effort of doing neither left her staring at him in dumb horror.

A flicker of remorse showed in his eyes. 'I didn't realise who you were yesterday, until you'd gone.'

At least he had some idea of the position he'd put her in. And if this wasn't quite an apology, at least it wasn't a declaration of out-and-out war.

'I didn't catch your surname.' She flushed, remembering that Adrian had kicked him before he'd had a chance to say it.

'Let me help you with the bag.' He was suddenly closer than she'd like. 'I know you've got to be hurting.'

Cori thought about telling him she could manage, but it was much too late for that. He'd already seen the bruises. She'd already betrayed far more about herself than he needed to know, and then she'd allowed herself to fanta-sise about those innocent-as-sin blue eyes. The detached professionalism which she'd intended to hit Dr Riley with this morning wasn't going to work.

'Thanks.' She grabbed at the strap of her bag, trying awkwardly to lift it over her head, and he came closer still to help, grimacing when he felt its weight.

'How did you get here?' It was probably just concern on his part, but Cori couldn't help but feel there was an edge of criticism to the question. She took a breath, lacing her answer with a smile.

'By taxi. If I'm going to be reckless, I'd prefer to do it the easy way.'

Taking the gamble of joking with him didn't come off well. He seemed about to smile and then reconsidered, turning abruptly to lead the way past the reception desk. Cori followed him along a snaking corridor, her eyes fixed on his back, trying not to count the number of ways that she might be in disgrace.

He threw open a door. 'We've set a room aside for you.'

'Thanks...' Cori caught her breath. The health authority scheme, linking art therapists with local hospitals, had pro-duced a set of guidelines that stipulated a separate room, but most of the therapists in her group had been given a large cupboard at best. Tom might not approve of her presence, but he'd given her a bright and airy room, with two large tables to work at and a small seating area in one corner.

'This is...' Perfect. Wonderful. Suddenly it was quite unbelievable. 'Are there any limitations on when I can use the room?'

'Nope. It's all yours for eight weeks.' The breath of a

smile played around his lips. 'That's what the guidelines requested.'

'The guidelines asked for more than anyone expected to get.' Cori looked around. 'This is perfect, thank you.'

His nod indicated that he'd heard, but conveyed nothing else. 'I have a meeting in a minute, so I hope you don't mind if I leave you to it. I'll get Maureen, the unit administrator, to show you around and then perhaps you can use today to get settled. It would be good if you could draw up a list of proposals for the kinds of activities you want to run, as well.'

She already had a list of proposals. Okay, so she hadn't seen the space she was going to be using, but she'd made sure to include options that covered almost anything from a broom cupboard to Buckingham Palace. But Tom seemed to be intent on getting out of the room as quickly as possible and was already halfway to the door. Taking a breath and thinking first, before she said anything rash, was the thing to do now.

'Thank you. Maureen, you say...?'

Was that a smile? Maybe he was congratulating himself at not having to bother with her any more this morning. 'Yeah. She probably won't be in yet, but I'll leave a note on her desk. If you stay here, she'll find you.'

'Okay, thanks.'

This time there definitely was a smile. As swift as it was melting, it sent warmth tingling through her followed by a sudden, empty feeling of loss as it was withdrawn. She almost choked.

'Coffee machine's in the main office. Help yourself.' He was gone. Taking with him his smile, the fresh scent that Cori had tried not to notice, and any hope that she might have had of winning him around at their first meeting.

She sat down with a bump, wincing as she did so. This morning hadn't quite gone as she'd intended, but she was still here. And she was still in with a chance of finding out exactly what Tom had against her being here, and of changing his mind.

Not so long ago, the only thing expected of Tom when a pretty young woman arrived on the unit was that he would turn on the charm and ask her to dinner. But then Dr Shah had suffered a heart attack, and it had fallen to Tom to keep the unit running while he was away on extended leave.

It was a mystery to him that Cori was even here. He'd seen the bruises and knew that she must be hurting like hell. It wasn't as if there was any hope of a job once her eight weeks in the hospital were up. Funding had been withdrawn, and the only reason this placement hadn't been cancelled was that it had been considered too late to stop it. But she seemed determined, and it was his responsibility to provide her with as many opportunities as he could.

Thankfully Maureen was already at her desk, reviewing the contents of her handbag before she started her day. At least he could send someone else to provide Cori with the welcome that he'd entirely failed to give.

'Was that the new art therapist I saw you with?' Maureen dispensed with the usual *Good morning* and *Did you have a nice weekend?*

'It was. Do you still have time to show her around?'

'Of course. What have you said to her?'

'That I'd see if I could find you...'

'So, in other words, you ducked the issue.'

'I know it looks a lot like that. Now I'm Acting Head of Department, I think I'm allowed to call it delegating.' He grinned at her and she rolled her eyes. Maureen had been in the department for twenty years and there was no one, including Tom, who hadn't been picked up and dusted down by her at one point or another in their career.

'I'll tell you now that I've no intention of playing good cop. Or bad cop, for that matter, if that's what you're asking.'

'I wouldn't dream of it.' He imagined that the woman he'd met yesterday in A and E would spot such a game a mile off, and probably outplay him. 'I just want you to keep an eye out for her. Let me know how she's doing.'

'And the better she does, the less you'll like it?' She looked at him thoughtfully. 'Does she know that?'

'It's not as simple as that...'

'No. Nothing ever is.' Maureen got to her feet, pulling her jacket straight in a no-nonsense motion. 'Just as long as I'm not the one who has to explain that to her.'

Tom Riley was almost certainly a better doctor than he was a boss. Cori considered the matter carefully as she tidied up the pens and paper from the afternoon's art session. It had been fun. Children from the ward had been joined by parents and siblings and more than one person had said that it was a great addition to the pastoral care that the unit provided. The only problem was that it hadn't been art therapy.

The next eight weeks might not be precious to Tom but they were precious to her and time was trickling away. A day, then two, now three...

As expected, Ralph and Jean had provided comfort food, followed by advice over the washing-up.

'You know this isn't your fault, don't you?' Ralph was soaping plates vigorously.

'That's how it feels.' She could share those fears with Ralph. He knew that was how she'd felt when she'd been a kid, rejected by one family after another. It had almost been too late by the time he and Jean had finally found her.

'So you'll be getting up at six in the morning to do the housework?' A smile played around Ralph's mouth. 'You want a hand with that?'

Cori chuckled. That was exactly what he had said when he'd found her in the kitchen, seven years old and trying to reach the switch for the washing machine, reckoning that if she made herself useful Ralph and Jean might keep her for a while. She'd liked their relaxed, cluttered household from the start and being allowed to stay had seemed like the first time a dream had ever come true for her.

'I think I've got it covered. I'm not going to be washing Dr Riley's socks.'

'Glad to hear it.' Ralph stacked more plates onto the drainer, his brow puckered in thought. 'So let me get this clear. There's an initial eight-week period, and if that's a success the post becomes permanent.'

'Yes, that's right. It's such a good opportunity, working with children, close to home. It's exactly the job I want.'

'And this Dr Riley doesn't want you. Why on earth did he agree to it in the first place?'

'That's the thing, he didn't. His predecessor, Dr Shah, agreed to it, and now this Dr Riley has got his reservations. I've emailed the scheme's supervisor to ask her why, but she's now on holiday. And I'm sure Dr Riley's avoiding me.'

'Is there anyone else you can talk to?'

'Only Maureen, the unit administrator. She's been really welcoming, but it's up to Dr Riley to refer specific patients on to me if I'm to do any clinical work. If he doesn't do that, then all I can do is general art sessions.'

'And you're taking that personally, eh?'

'How else can it take it? Every time I see him he either

rushes off before I can get to talk to him or he says he's busy and he'll get back to me.'

'Is he like that with everyone else?' Ralph frowned as he turned the problem over in his head.

'You saw what he was like with Adrian, he's fantastic with the kids. They all think he's the coolest doctor ever.'

'What about the other staff?'

'Everyone says he's great. That he always listens and is very fair about things. They seem to like him a lot better than Dr Shah. He was apparently pretty autocratic.'

The frightened child in her, who had blamed herself each time a fostering arrangement had fallen through, had been tugging at Cori's sleeve for the last three days. Keeping her behind after work, even though her sore ribs were screaming for a hot bath, working to make the best of the room she'd been given.

She'd succeeded. The children loved the room, and no one had been able to walk across the threshold without being tempted to touch at least something. The problem had been that Tom Riley hadn't yet found time to walk across the threshold. And that rejection outweighed every other expression of delight.

Ralph shook the suds from his hands, and wrapped his arm around her shoulders. 'There's no shame in saying this place isn't right for you, Cori. You don't have to prove yourself. They're the ones who have to be good enough for you.'

She hugged him tight. 'Thanks. Spoken like the best dad in the world.'

Ralph gave a small chuckle of pleasure. 'So what are you going to do, then? We're around at the weekend to help you with some more job applications, if you want to come over.'

It seemed like a plan. Since this job didn't seem to be

going too well, it would be good to keep all her options open. But she wasn't ready to give up on Dr Riley just yet.

'Thanks. I think I'll give it another week or so, though. I've still got a couple more things up my sleeve.'

It had been a long and busy week and all Tom wanted to do was go home, fling himself onto the sofa and think about nothing. Heading up the paediatric unit wasn't as easy as Dr Shah had made it look. But slowly he was cracking it. One problem at a time. One patient. One member of staff.

The light glimmering on his windscreen hadn't stood out amongst the other reflections from the overhead strip lighting in the car park. In truth, he'd been thinking hard about something else, and it wasn't until he'd flipped the central locking that Tom switched his attention to his car.

Perched on his windscreen wiper was a fairy. Actually, it was a bundle of scrunched-up silver wire, some sparkly fabric and a bit of tinsel. But the whole was a great deal more than its parts, and the resulting fairy leaned as if inspecting the exact spot where he was standing, her head tilted slightly in a questioning pose.

'What do you want?' Tom shot the creature a glare. It was a little late to start believing in fairies now. Particularly on a cold, wet Friday evening.

The fairy ignored him. Whatever she was doing here, it was clearly none of his business, even if she was sitting on his windscreen. Tom looked around, and saw that his car was the only one that sported an otherworldly being.

It was just a bundle of wire and gauze, which had somehow landed here by accident. The significance of its pose was a trick of the light. Tom reached for the fairy and then hesitated, as the bundle of wire and glitter seemed to scowl at him reproachfully. Its outstretched hand held a wand.

His gaze followed the direction in which the gently

glowing tip of the wand was pointing. The passage of car tyres over the concrete floor had scattered it a little, but the trail of glitter was still easy to see.

There was only one person who could have done this, and he'd been avoiding her all week. Slinging his briefcase into the back of his car, and giving the fairy one last baleful stare before he locked it in the glove compartment, he followed the trail of glitter that Cori had laid.

As soon as he stepped onto the frosty path outside the car park, Tom could see where he was headed. It was pretty much impossible not to notice the tiny lights, glimmering amongst the spreading branches of the tree that stood by the main entrance to the hospital. A nurse passed him walking in the other direction, holding a fairy in her hand, the little LED light at the tip of its wand glowing in the darkness.

When he got closer, he saw Cori leaning against the dark shadow of the tree trunk, her face lit up by the twinkle of lights in the branches around her. She did him the courtesy of not pretending to be surprised to see him.

'People usually find that leaving a note on my desk works.' Tom was trying hard not to be enchanted by this method of catching his attention.

'Do they?' She grinned up at him, her eyes dark in the shadows. 'You seemed so very busy.'

He supposed he deserved that. Each day that he'd transferred his meeting with Cori onto his 'to do' list for tomorrow, it had been easier to put it off. When Friday had come, the difficult problem of what exactly he should say to her had seemed quite naturally to fit into next week's timetable instead of this week's.

'Okay.' He was in the wrong and if it had been anyone else Tom would have apologised. But an apology was meaningless unless one intended to change in some way, and right now changing his mind was out of the question. 'So what's the point of all this?'

She folded her arms across her chest, looking up at him. 'You're my point.'

A sudden breathless feeling seemed to spread heat across his chest. 'How, exactly?'

Cori shrugged. 'I know you have your reservations about my effectiveness in the unit...' A little quiver in her voice told Tom that this mattered to her.

'I have no doubts whatever about your effectiveness.' Tom glanced at the fairies, cavorting around them in the tree. Some touch of magic had turned them from confections of wire and glitter into personalities, each one thrilling with life. There was a small group obviously arguing about something. Some preened themselves, and others beckoned watchers closer, looking no doubt to cast some kind of spell on them.

'Then...what?' She stared at him, nonplussed.

It seemed that she needed to hear him say this. He couldn't for the life of him think why, but if it would get her off his back, then he was more than happy to oblige. 'Look, Cori, your CV is very impressive, your work is great and the kids are enjoying it...'

'You haven't seen any of my work yet.' She looked ready for a staring match. From somewhere, the craving to respond hit him, the urge to look deep into those violet eyes, and break down all her defences.

'I do take a look around the unit once in a while. And I quite often talk to my patients, as well.' Tom resisted the temptation to add that talking to children was a damn sight easier than navigating the uneasy waters of adult office politics. 'I can see that you've been making a difference...'

'And making a difference is a good thing, isn't it?'

Tom wondered if she was deliberately playing dumb, or

she really didn't know. Surely she knew that the funding had been cut. It was impossible that no one had told her.

'You have the potential to be a real asset for the unit, Cori. But now that we have no funding for a long-term appointment, and it's just this eight weeks...'

She was staring at him as if he'd just grown a pair of wings and was about to flutter off into the branches with the fairies. Her mouth formed an 'O', and she covered it with her gloved hand. 'So... There's no permanent post... after these eight weeks are over?'

'No. I'm sorry. Once your work placement is finished, there are no plans for any permanent post until next year at the earliest. Didn't the scheme supervisor tell you that?'

She shook her head and abruptly turned away, as if there was something she wanted to hide from him. Disbelief, maybe. Tears? Anger? It was difficult to say, and, if he was honest, he would rather not have to deal with any of those emotions. He should go now, let her think about things over the weekend and they could talk again about what she wanted to do on Monday morning.

'Hey, Tom! What's going on? Can anyone join in?' A voice came from behind him and Tom turned to see a couple of off-duty nurses, one of whom was trying to draw his attention to a little girl, transfixed by the lights in the tree and trying to escape her father's grip on her hand. It seemed that they had just come from A and E, because the man also carried a younger child with a bulky dressing on her arm.

Cori had already seen them and was moving towards them. 'Would they like to come and take a look?' She spoke to the man first, and when he nodded she bent down to the little girl at his side. 'If you want, you can take a fairy home.'

The answer to that was a clear and overwhelming yes.

She led the little girl under the sparkling canopy, and her father followed, the child in his arms reaching up with her uninjured hand to touch the fairies. It was touching, heart-warming, and Tom wanted to be a part of the magic that Cori was able to create, more than he could say. Which was exactly why it would be much better if he went home. Now.

CHAPTER THREE

NOT SO FAST. Cori could see Tom out of the corner of her eye, pulling his car keys out of his pocket. She'd spent all of yesterday evening making fairies, and her lunchtime today attaching the little LED lights to the tips of their wands. He'd found his way here, and if he thought he was going anywhere before they talked this out, he was mistaken.

'Dr Riley. We need some help here.'

She called over to him, indicating the child beside her. Tom turned, his eyes narrowing in an indication that he knew full well that she wasn't playing fair, and she grinned at him in reply.

He moved across the grass towards her with all the affability of a tiger caught in a trap. He lifted the child up in his arms so she could reach the fairy that she wanted, never taking his gaze from Cori's face.

'Thank you.' The little girl responded to a prompt from her father and thanked him, and Tom's face broke into the kind of smile that Cori would have decorated the whole hospital with fairies for.

'You're very welcome.' He bent down, watching as the child inspected the fairy. 'What's her name?'

'Only *I* know it.'

Tom nodded gravely. 'Right. Well don't forget to take good care of her. She needs to have breakfast every morning.'

'Porridge?'

'Yep. I'm told that fairies are very partial to porridge. Particularly during the winter.'

The child nodded. 'Can Hannah have one?'

Tom allowed himself to be drawn into choosing and obtaining a fairy for the child with the injured arm. Before he was finished, Cori had given away another four, as hospital staff and visitors stopped to look at the tree.

'Dr Riley?' A man in a suit and overcoat was marching across the grass towards them. Tom turned away from the children, and the corner of the man's mouth twitched downwards.

'Now we're in for it...' He murmured the words as he passed behind Cori, moving forward to meet the man. 'Alan. Have you come to make a wish?'

It didn't look as if the man believed in fairies. Cori noticed that a couple of the nurses who'd been lingering under the tree had melted away, leaving the sparkling branches to those who were obviously not employed at the hospital and therefore not subject to the disapproval of its administrators.

'Just came to see what's going on.' Alan was looking round with an assessing gaze.

'Make-a-wish Friday.' Tom's smile would have cracked an iceberg, but he was obviously improvising, and Cori stepped forward. If anyone was going to get into trouble for this, then it should be her.

'It's all my...' She felt fingers close around the sleeve of her coat and Tom pulled her back a couple of steps.

'These are all Cori's creations. She's attached to the unit temporarily and she's been doing some stupendous work. We had some leftover fairies and I thought it was a shame for them to go to waste.'

'You're supervising this?'

'Absolutely. Can't have people wandering around hospital grounds making unsupervised wishes.'

Cori opened her mouth to speak and Tom turned to face her. For a moment his gaze met hers and she forgot what she was about to say.

'I suppose...' Alan looked around and gave a small shrug. 'There *is* a procedure to go through for anything like this in the hospital grounds, though.'

'Yes, I know. I apologise, but it was an off-the-cuff thing. Next time we'll go through the right channels.' Tom's gaze swung around to Alan, and for a moment it was touch-and-go as to who was going to outstare who. Then Alan backed down.

'No apologies needed, I'm sure. Good work...um...'

'Cori Evans.' Tom smiled beatifically in Cori's direction.

'Good work, Ms Evans. Thank you. You're the new art therapist?'

'*Temporary* art therapist.' The years when she'd moved from one foster home to another, before finding a home with Ralph and Jean, had taught Cori that the 'T' word was one to be both respected and feared. Knowing the difference between something that might work out and something that was strictly temporary was vital to one's own sense of self-worth.

'Did I mention that the unit could really do with someone on a permanent basis?' Tom broke in again.

'Several times.' Alan bestowed a hurried smile on Cori, and obviously decided it was time to retreat. Tom watched him go, his face impassive.

'I'm sorry.' She'd tried to get Tom's attention, and had ended up getting into hot water. And, unlikely as it might seem, it had been Tom who'd come to her rescue.

He shrugged. 'It's okay. Alan's all right, he just gets a

bit scratchy when you don't fill in the necessary forms. Next time you take anything out of the unit, let Maureen know. She'll notify the right people.'

'Yes. I'll do that.' There wasn't going to be a next time. This had been all about getting Tom's attention, finding out why he seemed so dead set against her working in the unit. And Cori had found out a great deal more than she'd wanted to know.

'Look…' He turned suddenly. In the darkness, his hair seemed every colour from blond to tawny. 'I thought that you knew that the funding for the art therapy scheme had been cut. I don't know who omitted to tell you that, but I intend to find out.'

'It's okay…'

'It's not okay.' He frowned.

'It will have been the scheme supervisor at the local health authority. She's been under a lot of stress recently, so I suppose she must have forgotten, and she's on holiday now so she hasn't responded to any of my emails.' Cori shrugged. 'Please. Leave it. I don't want to get her into trouble.'

'In that case, I'll deliver the reprimand to myself, for not making sure that you understood the situation.'

'No. Please, don't do that either. It won't change anything.' She could feel tears pricking at the sides of her eyes now, and hoped that the darkness would hide them from him. 'This is why you have your reservations about me doing clinical work in the unit, isn't it? You don't want me to start something when there's no chance of any follow-up.'

'Yeah. I just don't think it's fair to offer therapy to someone and have it stopped after only eight weeks. I'm sorry, Cori.' He seemed suddenly very close. Close enough to put his arm around her, and if he did that she would make a fool of herself and start crying.

'Don't...' She took a step backwards. 'There's no need to be sorry. You're right.' He was acting in his patients' best interests and Cori couldn't argue with that. But she couldn't just accept it either.

'Will you give me an hour? Please? Just one hour of your time.'

He shot her a melting look that seemed to say he understood all her hopes, all her fears. 'In all fairness I have to tell you that I can't change my mind. You're welcome to hold general groups and sessions on the unit, but I won't offer you anything more.'

'Maybe there's something else I can do... Please. Just an hour.' He hesitated, and Cori took her opportunity. 'What harm can it do to listen?'

He shook his head. Then he smiled, and suddenly she was looking at the Tom Riley who had such a special connection with the children under his care. The one who could make people feel that everything was all right with the world.

'Okay. But you come alone. No fairies.'

'Of course not. That would be an unfair advantage.'

He nodded. 'I don't have much time next week. But I'm dropping in to the hospital tomorrow and I'll be finished at about four. Will that suit you?'

'Four o'clock is fine.'

'Okay, I have your mobile number, I'll call you then.' He looked around at the fairies. 'What are you going to do with these?'

Cori shrugged. 'There doesn't seem to be any shortage of takers for them. I think I'll stop here for another fifteen minutes and give them away.'

'You don't want to save them for another time?'

She shook her head. 'Nah. I can always make more, and I think these all deserve a home now.'

'Having done what they were meant to do for tonight?'

He'd come uncomfortably close to the truth, but Cori wasn't about to admit it. 'You think this was all for you?'

'I'm not that self-centred. I think you want to be of benefit to the children, and to do that you need to catch my attention. And that you found a way to do that which also highlighted your own skills.'

Was that a compliment or a warning? Was he telling her he knew what she was up to and that he was more than a match for her? Before Cori could even begin to work it out, he was walking away.

Tom parked in the tree-lined avenue at the address that Cori had given him. A large Victorian mansion, converted into flats, stood back from the road. Running his finger down the row of names next to the door, he found Cori's and pressed the bell alongside it, hearing a chime sound from somewhere deep inside the house.

She answered almost immediately, wearing a padded coat that engulfed her small frame, accessorised with striped gloves, a scarf and a brightly coloured woollen beret, set at a rakish angle. Tom found himself wondering whether jeans and a leather jacket were quite right for the occasion. Somehow a suit would have made this outing feel more professional and less like a date.

'Is this thing you want to show me far?'

'We only have an hour, so we'll go by car.' Tom's gaze followed her pointing finger to a small, rather battered blue car. 'We could take mine, but the heater's broken...'

He imagined that the suspension was as old as the bodywork looked. And although it was nearly a week since he'd examined the bruises on her shoulder and hip, some of them had been deep enough to still be hurting her. 'We'll take mine. You can give me directions.'

She nodded, looking slightly relieved. 'Yes. More comfortable.'

As he opened the door for her, and she slid carefully into the passenger seat, the world suddenly felt right again. Working in the unit today had carried with it a sense of dislocation, as if something was missing, something that he had been doing his best to ignore. Now that Cori was in his car, Tom realised what that something had been.

'So what is it you want me to see?' They'd driven through a maze of back streets, until he'd lost his bearings.

'I'd rather it took you by surprise.' When he glanced across at her, her face had taken on an impish expression.

'Ah. So it would be wrong of me to try and guess.'

'Very wrong. Turn left here.'

They drew up outside a building that Tom recognised as the old town hall, which now housed a community centre and various offices. Cori led the way along a broken path that wound its way to the back of the building, and then down some metal steps into a gloomy passageway that led to the sub-basement space. Tom squinted at the metal plate on the door, recognising the name of a local charity working with families affected by domestic violence.

His heart felt as if it were stopping. How could she know? No one knew. His childhood was the one part of Tom's life that he kept strictly private.

'What's this?' His voice sounded distant, as if he'd left his body and was already halfway up the steps and out of there.

'I've been working here with some friends from art college. I want you to see what we've been able to do.' She pressed a rather ancient-looking buzzer on one side of the door.

'Your CV says you've been working at another hospital.' Suspicion clawed at him. If she was trying to gain his favour, by thinking she knew what made him tick, she was going about it in quite the wrong way.

'Yes, that's right. I was there for a year, covering for one of the therapists who was on maternity leave. I worked here at the weekends.' She turned to him, her face bright in the darkness. 'We finished up last Sunday. Or rather the others finished up. I was unavoidably detained elsewhere.'

So this was what she'd been doing when she'd fallen off the ladder. Before Tom could think about apologising for the suspicions he hadn't voiced, the door opened and warm light flooded out into the gloomy passageway.

'Cori.' The woman at the door hugged her gingerly. 'How are you doing?'

'Fine, thanks. I've been resting up.'

'Glad to hear it.' The woman turned a smile onto Tom, as if she suspected he'd probably had something to do with that. 'You're Dr Riley? Welcome. I'm Lena Graves, the centre's director.'

Lena motioned them both inside, into a small reception area. It was then that Tom realised why he was there.

CHAPTER FOUR

A FAINT SMELL of new paint still lingered in the place. Three
of the walls were painted cream and the fourth was a riot
of colour that stopped Tom in his tracks.

'Fabulous…' It was a glimpse into a world of pure fan-
tasy. Lushly painted trees and flowers formed the frame-
work for animals and birds, engaged in familiar, human
pursuits. In one corner, a group of hedgehogs was holding
a tea party. In another, flamingos were gossiping together.

The design was covered with clear plastic panels, running the length and height of the wall. 'These are to protect it?'

Lena chuckled. 'Not really.'

Cori picked up a marker pen from a box on the reception desk and handed it to him. 'You're supposed to draw
on it. Have a go.'

He almost didn't dare. 'And it wipes off?'

'That's the idea. I've wanted to do something like this
for a while, and Lena agreed to let us try it out here.'

'It's working well so far. The children love it. One little
guy spent all afternoon here yesterday. He drew a picture
of himself sitting in a chair next to the hedgehogs.' Lena
grinned. 'The staff like doing their thing with it too. At
the end of the day we just wipe it all down, ready for tomorrow's designs.'

The tip of the marker pen hovered over the smooth, clear surface. 'You're thinking too much.' He heard Cori's voice close behind him.

'Yeah. Guess I am.' Tom stepped back, putting the cap back onto the pen. 'What happens if someone...if the drawings the kids make become challenging?'

'Challenging to who? The people who draw, or the people who are looking?' She looked up at him thoughtfully. 'Does that matter?'

'It might. If it's disruptive.'

'This area's always supervised. And most of the children who come here with their parents are traumatised because of their family situations. I imagine that Lena will tell you that drawing isn't the most disruptive way of revealing that trauma.'

'Not by a very long chalk.' Lena grinned. 'Anyway, sometimes it's the ones who sit quietly in the corner, and can't bring themselves to reveal anything, who worry me the most.'

'As opposed to someone like me, who reveals everything by painting all over your walls?' Cori chuckled, nudging Lena.

'We're not getting into that. We'll be here all evening.' Lena turned to Tom. 'There's more I'd like to show you. Through here, when you're ready...'

'Yeah. Thanks.' Tom couldn't take his eyes off the huge painting. It was like Cori, disturbing and confronting and yet captivating. Something he wanted to touch, but he knew that once he did so he would be unable to conceal the feelings that had the power to destroy him if he let them have their way.

'He's the only one.' Lena shrugged, mouthing the words to Cori as Tom turned from the painting, walking briskly away from it. He was the only person, adult or child, who had stood in front of the wall art with a pen in their hand without making their own addition to the design, however tiny.

And it was Tom Riley, the man who was in charge of her future for the next seven weeks, who had turned out to be completely immune to the temptation to draw. The one man she wanted to impress, and her best shot at doing just that had left him cold.

Maybe he was just trying to be objective. To not get involved so that he could make a better decision. Cori held on to that thought, allowing Lena to usher him into the activities room.

He spent a while looking at everything. The child-sized painted chairs, each of which had an individual design snaking up the legs and across the back. The art table, which she had arranged like a sweet shop, different pens and paper displayed with an implicit invitation to touch, to pick up and to draw.

'We got the chairs from a recycling charity.' She had to say something to break the silence. 'Some of them were a bit rickety, but we fixed them up and painted them...' This morning it had seemed like a good idea to show him this. Now she was wondering whether she hadn't blown things completely.

'They're great.' Finally, he smiled. Not the conspiratorial, we-know-a-secret smile that she liked more than she cared to say, but it was something at least.

'The wall here is painted with a wipe-clean surface.' She ran her hand across the hard, white finish. 'It's a different experience from the one outside. A clean slate.'

He nodded. 'You're encouraging the kids to paint on the walls?'

Lena came to her rescue. 'Just this wall. This is an experiment too. If we find too much graffiti all over the place then we'll paint over it and put it down to experience.'

'It's a lot of effort just to paint over.'

'If we try something and it doesn't work, that's not wasted effort. We learn and do better the next time. Lena's been great in allowing us to experiment a bit.' Cori flashed a grin towards Lena, who nodded, encouraging her to go on. 'You wanted to see something where the benefits didn't rely on having an in-house art therapist. I think this is it.'

'And how much did all of this cost? Just a ballpark figure.'

Cori caught her breath. If he was going to dismiss it out of hand, surely he wouldn't have asked that.

'Cori's group is self-funding.' Lena stepped in again. 'We couldn't have afforded this on our budget.'

He turned to her. The approval in his eyes was breathtaking. 'How much?'

'I'd…have to work it out. I can supply you with figures, but… Well, I'd prefer it if you would come to see our fundraising operation.' Nothing ventured, nothing gained.

'You have an…operation?' He raised one eyebrow.

'Well, that might be a bit of an overstatement…' No. They did. And she was proud of it. 'Yes, we do. And when you've finished looking around here, I'd like you to see it.'

As they left the building and walked back to the car, the cold evening air on his face seemed to jolt Tom back into the here and now. 'Where are we going this time?'

'The High Street. You carry on down here, take a left and then keep going until you get to the traffic lights.' She settled herself into the passenger seat of his car and buckled the seat belt, clearly not inclined to give any more information about what he was going to see.

'Right.' He started the engine, wondering what she was going to come up with next.

There were no clues from the place she indicated as a parking spot, and he became more baffled as she led him into a bright, warm tea shop, bustling with activity. Sitting down at a table, she loosened her scarf and coat, and signalled to a waitress.

'Hi, Cori. Pot of green tea?'

'Yes, thanks. Tom…?'

At some point in the course of the afternoon she'd responded to his request to stop calling him *Dr Riley*. Tom couldn't remember quite when that had been, but it felt good, as if she'd acknowledged that he might be at least partially on her side.

'Earl Grey, please.' He settled back in his chair, looking around. 'You run a tea shop?'

'No, of course we don't. Where would we get the time to do that?' She grinned, jerking her thumb at the back wall. 'That's our fundraising operation.'

The wall was covered with canvases, ranging from tabletop height almost as far as the ceiling, jostling together in a chorus of colour. 'You painted all of these?'

'I wish. There are over a dozen of us in the group, and everyone contributes a few paintings. The tea shop displays them for us and gets ten percent of sales. It brings people in here and they have something to put on their walls. It's a mutually beneficial arrangement.'

'And you use the money to fund the work that you do for charities.'

'Yes. Charities, schools, hospitals…' That impish grin appeared again. 'Actually, we haven't done any hospitals. But we would, if we got the chance.'

Tom chuckled. 'Anywhere in mind?'

'No, not specifically. We're just open to the possibility.'

'I see.' He could think more clearly now. 'So can you tell me what all this has to do with art therapy?'

She laughed. 'I was wondering when you were going to ask me that.'

'It's the obvious question. As I understand it, art therapy is all about the process of engaging people in some kind of artistic pursuit in a safe environment, and working through the issues that it raises for them. I've only seen the first half of that process today.'

'It has its benefits, though.'

'I'm not denying that.' Tom nodded a thank-you as the waitress put a cup and saucer and a small teapot down in front of him. 'I think what you've done at the centre is fantastic. It's welcoming and inclusive, and at the same time it's challenging…'

'But you're right. It's not art therapy.' She flashed him a smile. 'It *is* sustainable, though, and it's helping to create a culture where users of the centre can use art to express themselves. I'd like to have a conversation with you about doing something of the sort in your department.'

This was something that she lived for, that set her alight, the way that medicine set Tom alight. And fire suited her. He wondered what it might be like to feel her heat flickering across his skin, warming him on a cold night.

'That's going to be a fairly lengthy conversation.'

'I hope so. And I imagine we'll have a few creative differences along the way. Are you up for it?'

Tom reminded himself that Cori would be working as a part of his team. The only fire that he should be sharing with her was the one that would temper their working relationship.

'I'm up for it.' His gaze found hers, and heat began to throb through his veins. 'There's one condition.'

'Okay.'

'I want to be sure that this is an arrangement that we can both benefit from. I imagine you've already got a few ideas about things that could be done in the unit?'

'One or two.' Her grin told him that it was more than one or two, but that she was planning on surprising him.

'In that case, I want a list of clearly defined benefits, to us and to you. I can't offer you any long-term prospects of employment, so I'd like to know how you feel the work you do will help your career after you leave us.'

Her eyebrows shot up, giving Tom the satisfaction of knowing that he was able to pull a few surprises out of the bag, as well. It seemed that working with Cori was not only going to be possible but more fun than he could have imagined.

'That's… Yes, that would be valuable for me.' She seemed to be ruminating on the thought. 'You know, you're not such a bad boss after all…'

'I'm a work in progress as a boss. I'm a much better doctor.' Tom held out his right hand. 'Do we have a deal?'

Her fingers brushed his, and then gripped tight. 'Yes. We have a deal.'

CHAPTER FIVE

WHEN TOM DREAMED that night, it wasn't of Cori, neither was it of his father. The jumbled landscape of his dreams rarely made any logical sense. He had been standing in front of the vivid wall painting but was shrunk to the size of a child, so that he was on the same level as the hedge-hogs' tea party. The creatures seemed to be moving, beck-oning to him, and he wanted to join in but his feet were stuck to the floor. He struggled, but whatever was binding him wouldn't let go.

He woke suddenly, an obscure feeling of relief accom-panying the realisation that he was in his own bed, in his own house. In his own life, away from the unpredictabil-ity of his father's temper. He could be who he wanted to be, someone who made a difference in the world instead of a frightened child, whose greatest desire was to make himself invisible so that no one would notice him.

Tom had never known what he might have done had his mother lived. But she'd died from cancer when he was twelve, and when Tom had got a place at medical school he'd been free to walk away from his father, without look-ing back. That freedom hadn't amounted to much at first, but he'd worked on it. Worked his way through the night terrors and the flashbacks that had started to haunt him, and the anger and grief that had surfaced as soon as he had begun to feel safe enough to feel anything.

And now Cori was beginning to chip away at the armour he'd so carefully put in place. He'd woken up in the middle of the night, too sleepy to realise what he was doing, and reached for Cori, wanting her to be there. And he didn't do that sort of thing. The acclaimed master of the romantic weekend break, he had only one rule, and that was that he never asked a woman back to his place. Keeping himself at a distance allowed him to be the man he wanted to be.

He got out of bed, stumbling towards the bathroom. Cori's particular brand of unpredictability might be very sweet, and a world away from his father's, but it still wasn't for him. The best thing—no, the *only* thing—to do now was to ignore that enchanting way of hers and the undoubted spark between them, and concentrate on how her eight weeks in the unit might benefit his patients.

Cori was now in no doubt that Tom had made up his mind to lead by example. On Monday he had wheeled a young patient into her room, introducing his parents to Cori, and had sat down with the boy to help him with paper and crayons for ten minutes. Three slightly older girls arrived, after Tom had reported the possibility that fairies might be on the premises, and a couple of boys came to enquire whether Tom's hint of intergalactic warriors was more than just an unfounded rumour.

By Thursday, the whole unit had been in receipt of the gossip concerning a long, and sometimes animated, meeting in the staff canteen at lunchtime the previous day. Tom had waved away anyone who had attempted to join them, and had spent more than an hour going through Cori's portfolio of photographs and suggestions.

And where Tom led, the rest of the unit followed. The staff began to automatically include the art room when telling patients' families about the facilities that the unit offered, and gradually it was becoming a hub of activity instead of a rarely visited outpost.

By Friday, the prospect of an hour on her own at lunch-time was a welcome respite. As the last of the children were taken back to the ward Tom's secretary appeared in the doorway.

'Hi, Rosie.'

'I brought you some tea.' Rosie held two mugs, which were obviously her excuse for coming to have a look around.

'Thank you, that's really nice of you.' Cori pulled out a chair. 'Will you join me?'

'Thanks.' Rosie was small, blonde and very precise, and dusted the chair before she sat down. 'How does this all work?'

'Art therapy, you mean?'

'Yes. It looks as if it's just painting sessions at the moment.'

The words hurt, but that wasn't Rosie's fault. Cori forced a smile. 'I'm only here for eight weeks. There's a limited amount I can do in the time.'

Rosie nodded. 'I'll mention it to Tom.'

Cori bit back the temptation to say that she'd already mentioned it. Rosie seemed to like her position as secretary to the head of department, and clearly felt that a measure of Tom's authority automatically devolved to her.

'Thanks. Although it's really just the way that things are.'

'You'd be surprised what Tom can do when he puts his mind to it.' Rosie tucked a stray lock of hair behind her ear. 'I haven't been working for him for long, but I've really got to know what makes him tick.'

What made Tom tick? It had been a question that had taken up more of Cori's time than it should have, and it appeared that Rosie had cracked it. Cori dismissed the thought that perhaps Rosie just *thought* she'd cracked it as unfair.

'How long have you been working for Tom?' She supposed she should show some interest.

'Not long, just a couple of months. Dr Shah's secretary used to look after Tom as well, but she's gone on maternity leave. I'm the one with the most seniority in the department after her.'

'So you got the promotion?'

'Yes. I don't think that Terri's coming back after her maternity leave. I heard her talking to Maureen...' Rosie gave a little self-satisfied nod, as if to indicate that she knew more than Cori about the internal workings of the department.

Silence seemed like the best option at this point, and Cori sipped her tea.

'So what *do* you do, exactly?'

That she had an answer for. Cori grinned, pushing a pile of paper closer to Rosie. It was beautifully printed, with blue and gold swirls, and she'd been keeping it for something special, but it seemed that the situation warranted it.

'That's gorgeous.' Rosie picked up a sheet. 'Textured...'

'Feel nice?' Cori moved the pile away from Rosie. One sheet was enough to make her point.

'Yes, it does. You've used it for folding... That's lovely.' Rosie nodded towards a paper crane that Cori had suspended from the ceiling.

'You want me to show you?'

Cori picked up a square of rough paper, and Rosie care-

fully followed the folds that she made. They worked together until the blue and gold bird was finished and lay
in Rosie's hands.

'See, it feels good to make something.' Cori smiled at
her.

'Yes, it does. And this is what you do?'

'No, it's the start of what I do. Painting, drawing, making things are all ways of relaxing, and feeling safe about
expressing ourselves. It helps people talk about the things
that they sometimes can't talk about otherwise.'

'So you're practising on me?' Rosie flushed a little.

'No. Just making a paper crane. I'm on my lunch break.'

'Okay. Can I take this?'

'Of course. You made it. Want to help me with some
more?' Cori pushed the cheaper paper towards Rosie. One
blue-and-gold crane was enough, and she couldn't afford
a whole flock of them.

'Yes, I've got half an hour.' Rosie took a sheet of paper
and started folding. 'Then I'll have to go. I usually give
Tom's office a tidy up when he's out of the way as he
doesn't like it when I do it when he's around. He's called
a meeting about new projects in the department.'

'Really? The meeting's in half an hour?' Perhaps this
was what Rosie had been supposed to tell her all along,
and she'd just got sidetracked.

'No, it's already started. That's where everyone is.'
Rosie smiled. 'Apart from us. Makes a nice change to
have a free lunch hour.'

The lump that had formed suddenly in Cori's throat
made words out of the question. She'd rather hoped that
she might be a contributor to at least one new project in
the department. And yet Tom had excluded her from this
meeting. Maybe he'd decided that he was going to turn
down the proposals she'd presented on Wednesday and

had resumed his earlier policy of avoiding her rather than breaking the bad news.

'He should do something like this...' Rosie was still talking, seemingly unaware that she'd lost her audience. 'It would do him good. He's very tense.'

'Uh?'

'Tom. He's very tense. It's not surprising, really, he's got such a lot of responsibility now. Lots of people don't notice because he hides it. I do, though, because I suffer from tension myself.'

Cori concentrated on the paper folding. Maybe Rosie would get the hint and shut up for a minute.

Not any time soon. Rosie admired her second crane and reached for a new piece of paper. 'Of course, sometimes he needs saving from himself.'

Cori didn't reply. Much as she might have liked it to be, saving Tom from himself wasn't her own special mission. She knew that.

'I'll bet no one's really mentioned it, but you should know.' Rosie leaned towards Cori confidingly. Something about the gesture seemed to indicate that this was what she'd really come to say, and that the tea and the interest in her work had just been polite preliminaries.

What if this was something she really did need to know and not just idle gossip? 'Yes?'

Rosie moved closer, obviously keen to unburden herself of this particular piece of information. 'You know, don't you, that he has...a reputation.'

Cori bit back the temptation to ask what Rosie meant. It was quite obvious from the look on her face that she was talking about Tom's love life. 'Really?'

That was enough to open the floodgates. 'Yes. I'm surprised no one else has mentioned it. Tom's very charming, well, I imagine you've noticed that already, and he dates loads of women. It never lasts, though.'

It wasn't her business, and it actually wasn't Rosie's either. But short of putting her fingers in her ears and singing loudly, it seemed that there was no way that Cori was going to be able to avoid hearing this.

'He always seems quite friendly with them, and they never seem to talk about it. That doctor down in A and E, Helen Kowalski, do you know her?'

Cori remembered vaguely that the first doctor who Adrian had seen had been called Kowalski, and that it had been her who'd called Tom. She decided not to encourage Rosie. 'No, I don't think I do.'

'Well, she's very pretty. Beautiful, actually, with very nice skin. She and Tom dated for a short while, a couple of years ago. She's with someone else now, I heard they were getting engaged...' Rosie's brow puckered slightly as if she was making a mental note to check on that piece of information. 'Anyway, it was all very civilised and Helen never said a word about what had happened. They still seem perfectly friendly...'

'That's...very professional.' Clearly Tom liked beautiful women who knew how to keep their mouths shut. The thought that the second characteristic probably ruled out anything much happening between Tom and Rosie was needlessly unkind but Cori couldn't help it.

'Oh, yes. He's always very professional. He's never been anything other than very professional with me.' Rosie's look invited Cori to answer the unasked question.

'Um... Yes, absolutely. Completely professional...with me.' Cori tried not to think about the smouldering look that Tom seemed to save for moments when they were alone together. *He* probably couldn't help that.

Rosie nodded, a hint of triumph in her smirk. Clearly

this had been on her mental list of things to find out and the answer pleased her in some unspecified way. 'I suppose I'd better be getting on. Can I take the cranes I made? They'd look nice hung up by my desk.'

'Yes, of course. Help yourself.'

Rosie picked up all the folded paper birds, those that Cori had made as well as her own, and made for the door, leaving her empty teacup behind on the table. Cori stared at it, as if it might contain some clue as to what had just happened.

But no. Undoubtedly the lipstick mark on the rim contained Rosie's DNA, but that wasn't a great deal of use. It might feel as if the Tom Riley who had been haunting her dreams for the last two weeks had just been stolen from her, but no actual crime had been committed here.

The one redeeming thing was that she hadn't shown her own hand. She hadn't made a fool of herself over a man who was apparently just as unreliable as he was good-looking.

Cori closed her eyes, breathing slowly and deeply. Okay. She knew three things. Tom had excluded her from a meeting that concerned her, which pretty much everyone else in the unit had been invited to. That hurt. Second, it seemed he had something of a reputation. That ought not to hurt, because it really wasn't any of her business. And, third, she'd just been warned off by his secretary.

Tom slipped his coat from the hanger, slinging it over his arm. Today had been a good day, and everything was right with the world. There was no requirement for fairies or trails of glitter this Friday. He'd seen that the light was on in the room that Cori had made her own, and that was all he needed to go to her.

'May I buy you a coffee?' She was sitting at the table,

staring at a child's painting. When she looked up at him her eyes were cool, like the blue waters of the Mediterranean at night.

'No...thanks. Would you come here a minute? There's something I'd like to show you.'

Something serious, from the look on her face. Tom let the door swing closed behind him and walked over to where she was sitting.

'It might be nothing.'

'Which implies it might be something.' He threw his jacket across the back of a chair and sat down.

'You see this? I've just noticed it...' She slid the painting she'd been studying towards him.

'Yes.'

'See how it slants? And there's a gap, here.' She swept her hand across the paper to indicate what she meant.

'Yes. Does that concern you in any way?' As far as Tom could see, it was simply a child's painting.

'Well, I don't know whether this is something that's already been picked up, I haven't seen the medical notes. But I think that this child has some kind of difficulty on his left side. Maybe his eye or in co-ordinating his left hand with what he sees.

Tom glanced at the name, written in Cori's clear hand in the corner of the painting. 'That's not something I'm aware of. Peter's broken leg is the result of him skidding and falling over on some ice.' He looked again at the painting. It did look a little lopsided but, then, Peter was only seven, and to Tom's untutored eye it was pretty much what he'd expect from a child his age.

Out of the corner of his eye he saw her straighten next to him. 'Okay. I'd like to have it put onto his notes, though, just in case. For reference...'

'There's no need for that.'

'I think there is.' Cori was obviously steeling herself for a confrontation, and Tom was snared by the temptation to play devil's advocate. Watching her defend the children in her care always gave him a kick.

'There's no need because I'm going to take a look at him right now.' Tom imagined he'd get plenty more chances to fight with Cori, without manufacturing one now, and got to his feet, snatching up his coat. 'Coming?'

She should have known that Tom's unreliability wouldn't extend to the children in his care. He swept into his office, throwing his coat and briefcase onto the chair, taking off his jacket and loosening his tie, the way he always did before he went onto the ward. Opening his desk drawer, he rummaged for a moment, before pulling out a penlight, and then turned quickly, almost bumping into her on his way out.

'Sorry...' They both moved the same way at the same time to avoid each other, and he muttered an apology, frowning when Cori tried to move out of his way and ended up blocking his path again.

When he took her by the shoulders she realised that she was shaking. He moved her gently to one side and led the way out of his office. She followed, almost running to keep up with him, and slid to a stop as he slowed suddenly before entering one of the wards.

Tom's relaxed gait revealed nothing of the purpose that he'd showed just a moment ago. On the wards he was always relaxed and ready to talk to anyone.

'Hey, Peter.' The boy grinned up at him, and Tom shot one of his conspiratorial smiles back, before turning his attention to Peter's mother, who was sitting next to his bed.

'Sarah, this is Cori.' Tom had given every indication of having forgotten that she was there, and Cori jumped

when she heard her name mentioned. 'She's an art therapist attached to the unit.'

'Hi.' Peter's mother turned to Cori. 'Are the folded paper
dinosaurs your work?'

'Mainly Peter's. I just helped.'

'Thank you.' Sarah nodded a smile of appreciation towards Cori, before turning to Tom. His nonchalant attitude
had fooled Peter into assuming that the only reason for
their presence there was to discuss dinosaurs, but Sarah's
instincts were a little sharper.

'I'd like to take a quick look at Peter's eyes. Just to make
sure everything's okay.'

'His eyes? Why wouldn't his eyes be okay?'

'We've noticed that he doesn't seem to see as well out
of his left eye.' Tom was watching Sarah, gauging her reaction. Caring for her, just as much as he cared for her son.

'Is that a problem?' Worry lines were spreading across
Sarah's face, like hairline cracks on a vase.

'I'm just making sure.' Tom smiled at her reassuringly,
flipping through Peter's notes. 'You said that he didn't hit
his head at all.'

'Not as far as I know. It all happened so quickly.'

'Yes. The A and E team examined him pretty thor-
oughly, and there's no mention of any bumps.' Tom focused his grin on Peter. 'What do you say we take another
quick look, eh?'

He seemed to evoke the same relaxed magic as when
he had examined Adrian. A few jokes, a little kindness,
and the impression that he had all the time in the world.
Cori saw that, with as little fuss as possible, Tom's attention strayed from Peter's eye to his left hand.

Turning, he summoned a nurse and Cori stepped back
from the bed. Tom gave some instructions and the nurse
hurried away. Then he rose, drawing the curtains around

Peter's bed. Brightly coloured curtains, which effectively told Cori that she wasn't wanted there any longer. She was on the outside, and anyone who mattered was on the inside.

She looked around the small ward, wondering whether it might be acceptable to go and sit with one of the other children and wait, to see what happened next, but all of them already had visitors. There was nothing else to busy herself with, and Cori was pretty sure that if she returned to the art room and stayed there to wait for Tom to come and find her, she'd be there all night. She wasn't needed any more and that was that.

This kind of thing happened all the time in hospitals. How many times had she initiated something at the last place she'd worked without getting to see the outcome? Working on her own in a small unit, rather than as part of a large team of therapists, she'd hoped that things might be different here, but that obviously wasn't the case.

What really hurt was Tom's attitude. She wasn't able to trust him but she wanted so much to do so. It just wasn't fair that he could ignore her so easily, and yet everything he did seemed to burn itself into her consciousness like a brand.

Cori marched back to her room and pulled on her coat, winding her scarf around her neck so vigorously that she almost choked herself. It was Friday evening, for goodness' sake. She was supposed to be getting ready for the weekend. Picking up her bag and resolving to do just that, she marched out of the unit.

CHAPTER SIX

WHEN SHE OPENED the door, and saw Tom standing on the doorstep, the smile slid from her face. Not a good sign. Maybe Saturday afternoon was a bad time to call, but he owed her an apology, and since Cori hadn't been around to receive it that morning Tom had decided to deliver it to her doorstep instead.

'Hi. You're in.' Of course she was in. How could she answer the door if she wasn't? Tom wondered if he sounded as tongue-tied as he felt.

'Yes. I'm in.'

Right. That was that one settled. On to the next thing. 'I just popped round on the off chance. I've been at work this morning.'

'Okay.' Her face betrayed nothing.

'I came to apologise. For leaving you hanging yesterday evening.'

She shrugged, her shoulders the only part of her body that divulged any clue to what she was thinking. 'No apology necessary. You were busy with Peter.'

'Yes. I thought you might like to know how he's getting on.'

His one last-ditch attempt at reaching her worked like a charm. Cori stepped back from the doorway.

'Yes, I would. Come in, I was about to make some coffee.'

'I don't want to disturb you if you're in the middle of something.' For the first time it occurred to Tom that she might not be on her own, that there might be someone she shared her Saturday afternoons with. Those entrancing eyes, the smile that had made him feel that she was somehow his couldn't have failed to go unnoticed by other men.

'No. I was doing some painting but I don't seem to be able to get it this afternoon.' Finally she smiled at him. 'Some days it's better just to leave it alone.'

He couldn't have left if he'd wanted to now. Tom stepped across the threshold and followed her along the hallway to her own front door, which was propped open by a large piece of stone that had been hewn in half to reveal a crystal inside. She nudged the doorstop out of the way with her foot and closed the door behind them.

It was hardly puzzling that he was beginning to find the scent of paint erotic, but it was disconcerting. Being at the mercy of his senses like this was not something that Tom liked to encourage in himself. But Cori... It was impossible not to let her presence flood over him. Like warm syrup. Or iced water. Whatever she did seemed to provoke in him an exaggerated reaction of either pleasure or pain.

She took his jacket, hanging it up in the narrow hallway, and led him through to a large, open-plan room which incorporated a small kitchen in one corner and a hotchpotch of furniture, most of which was probably second-hand. In the curve of a large bay window stood an easel, tilted towards the light so that it was impossible to see what the canvas on it showed.

Somehow, despite the fact that nothing matched, there was a feeling of harmony about the room. It was a bright, peaceful place, which calmed Tom's senses.

'So how is Peter?' She flipped open one of the kitchen cupboards and took out two mugs.

'He has a small tear in his retina. That's why he left a blank spot in his painting; he couldn't see that part of the paper.'

She whirled around suddenly to face him. 'Will his sight deteriorate?'

'Hopefully not. It's classified as an emergency and he had surgery this morning. I went in to be with him and talk him through it, and the ophthalmic surgeon is very pleased with the way things went.'

'Was it a result of his fall?'

'We don't think so. It seems to be a pre-existing condition. That's often a problem with diagnosing children, they don't always say when something's wrong, they just work around it.'

She set the mugs down with a clunk onto the kitchen counter. 'So I was right in coming to you?'

'Are you saying that you were considering *not* raising a concern about a patient because you might be mistaken?' Tom shot her a deliberately confrontational look.

'No, of course not.' The little toss of her head made him smile. 'Why, were you considering not doing anything about it because I might be mistaken?'

'Not for a moment.'

Now that was cleared up he could get to what he'd come here for. 'My apology...'

'Yes?' Suddenly she had him pinioned with her gaze. This feeling of powerlessness was something he'd avoided his whole life. Tom swallowed down a sudden and completely irrational urge to run.

'I came to apologise for offering you coffee and then leaving you standing there.'

Surprise flared in her expression momentarily, before she covered it up. 'That's okay. I didn't even notice.'

Perhaps she had and perhaps she hadn't. In any case, she

seemed much better disposed towards him than she'd been five minutes ago. 'You had more important things to do.'

'Yeah, I did. That doesn't mean I can't apologise.'

'Apology accepted. I'm just glad that I could be of *some* use in the department.' There was hurt in her eyes, and this time she didn't bother to cover it up.

'What's the matter, Cori? Last week you were very insistent on telling me exactly what you thought. This week you seem to be dropping hints.'

'Things change.'

She turned away from him, frowning at a small red coffee machine that stood on the counter. Tom settled himself on the high stool that sat next to the divider between the kitchen and the living space. Whatever had changed between last week and this week, he wasn't moving until he found out what had happened.

She was looking suspiciously at the coffee machine, as if it was about to blow up. It looked new, although it was difficult to tell because everything was so clean it all looked as if it hadn't been used yet.

'It won't bite, you know.' Tom folded his arms.

'No, I know. I had it for Christmas, and I'm not quite sure...' She was pressing each one of the buttons on the machine in turn.

She was normally so practical, so capable that it was unexpected to see her conquered by something as simple as a coffee machine. Tom couldn't help grinning. 'Have you got some capsules?'

'Yes. My brothers bought me some to go with it.' She flipped one of the cupboards open and Tom peered inside to see four unopened boxes of coffee.

'Which do you want?' He assumed she'd looked at the outside of the boxes at least.

'I'll have what you're having.'

Tom opened the box that contained the strongest brew, reckoning there was a good chance he was going to need it. Reaching across her to plug in the machine, he switched it on and dropped a capsule into the holder. Cori retreated to one of the high stools, seemingly content to let him get on with it, and Tom filled the machine's reservoir with water.

'You don't cook all that much?'

She didn't reply and Tom took that as a *no*. Anyone even vaguely interested in cooking generally didn't have a coffee machine for two months without at least reading the instructions and working out how to use it.

'Espresso? Or cappuccino?'

'Um. Espresso.'

He suspected that she'd chosen the option that sounded easiest. 'Cups?'

'There are some smaller cups in the top cupboard...' She was watching him steadily, as if waiting for him to do something. Tom finished making the coffee, setting hers in front of her.

'Would you be able to have some sessions with Peter next week?' He leaned back against the kitchen counter, taking a sip of his espresso.

'He's not having specific therapy for that eye?' Her face still showed no emotion.

'Yes, it's all arranged. But eye operations can be very difficult for kids, and he already has a relationship with you.'

'I could... I mean, I'd *like* to talk to him about it...' She seemed almost hesitant in asking.

'I did think that you might want to see things through with him.' If she didn't, he was going to drink his coffee, go home, and think hard about how he could have mis-judged her so badly.

'Yes, I would. Thanks. I won't wait until Monday, I'll

go and see him tomorrow if that's all right with you.' She
smiled at him, and suddenly it looked as if he was going
to stay.

Ridiculous. Crazy. Just because Tom had arrived on her
doorstep, shown himself to be equal to the coffee machine,
and dropped a few crumbs to salve her wounded pride,
it didn't mean that he was to be trusted. He was still excluding her. And although Rosie's assessment of him was
probably not coming from an entirely rational place, Cori
believed her.

So why did she feel like flinging herself into his arms?
Ripping his clothes off and dragging him through to her
bedroom? No, actually taking his clothes off very slowly
would be a lot better...

Cori dismissed the thought. He'd been so enthusiastic
about their plans for the art room and now it seemed he'd
dismissed them out of hand, without telling her why. If he
could reject her so easily, she should be more careful about
what she wished for where Tom was concerned.

She wouldn't allow herself to fantasise about him. Temporary families, temporary jobs, temporary lovers... None
of them were worth breaking her heart over.

'So what *is* the matter?' He was regarding her steadily,
giving her that *everything's okay* look that he gave the kids,
only this was the grown-up, X-rated version that was melting her insides and making her tremble.

'Nothing...'

'And since you don't trust me enough to tell me, then
you're obviously not going to trust me enough to confirm
if I guess correctly.'

'That doesn't necessarily follow.'

'So there *is* something.'

She may as well say it. She wasn't being petty, she was

a professional who reacted with her head. 'Okay. Well, I would have hoped that if you were calling a meeting about the unit's new projects, it might have been an obvious move to invite me.'

He stiffened suddenly, his eyes darkening with something that looked like anger. 'Who told you?' He held his hand up. 'No. Actually, don't tell me. I think I already know.'

'I'm not a sneak. Anyway, a department meeting is no big secret. And I have skills and expertise that can help you. I thought we'd agreed on that.' She could feel her heart pounding in her chest. This was where it all broke apart. Tom couldn't deny that he'd excluded her, and now that it was all out in the open she couldn't just meekly go along with it.

'Yes, we did. Which was exactly why you weren't at that meeting, because we could hardly talk about you if you were sitting right there.'

'You talked about me?' Cori wasn't sure whether she liked the sound of that or not. She walked over to the sink with her empty cup, to cover her confusion.

'Yes.' He moved his weight from the counter top behind him and took a step towards her. 'I said that I thought the unit had been given a unique opportunity, and that we should grab it with both hands. I said that your skills had the potential to make a measurable improvement in the services we offered our patients and their families.'

'Ah...' Perhaps it was her turn to apologise.

'I also said that I thought we should consider very carefully how much money we could raise in the next few weeks to finance some of the proposals that you made to me on Wednesday.' He seemed to be getting closer.

'You... I told you that the artists' group is self-funding.'

'Yes, you did.' He was definitely closer now. Close

enough to stretch out his arms either side of her and plant his hands on the edge of the sink behind her. 'Your group works hard for its funding. I think it behoves us to work equally hard to help raise money for work that you're offering to do at the unit.'

'I...' He was far too near for anything other than honesty now. The whole truth and not just part of it. 'I've made myself look like an idiot, haven't I?'

'No. I can see how it must have looked to you. I've made some preliminary enquiries with the hospital's building maintenance group, and it seems that it's my decision as to whether we go ahead or not. But I felt that I should at least discuss it with Dr Shah.'

'And you didn't want to tell me about it until you had.'

'I've spoken to him on the phone, and he was very enthusiastic. I'm going to see him at home tomorrow afternoon to show him your proposals. I don't think he's going to disagree with me.'

'Thank you, Tom.' Cori tried to avoid his gaze but couldn't. 'I've misjudged you.'

'Of course you did. How could you have done anything else when I've consistently neglected to discuss things with you?'

'You... It would be wrong to promise something you couldn't deliver.'

'Yeah. That's my excuse.' He was very close now, and his eyes promised something that Cori knew for certain he could deliver. In full, and then some. All she had to do was reach out.

She stood on her toes, brushing her lips against his cheek. 'Thank you. For everything you've done.'

'You're welcome. I don't suppose you'd like to do that again?'

'This?' She kissed his cheek again.

'Yeah.' He didn't move his hands from the counter top, but dipped his head to touch his lips to her forehead. All that Cori could think about was making this real. Letting go of the pretence and doing the one thing she wanted to do. She slid her hand over the soft wool of his sweater, up to the neck of his shirt. At the first touch of her fingers on his skin she heard his uneven intake of breath.

When she curled her arm around his neck, pulling him down towards her, he drew her in close, making sure that she felt his body against hers before she had a chance to feel his lips. He wanted her. The knowledge spilled into her like a bright light penetrating a very dark place. He wanted her.

His kiss told her that too. The way he took it slowly, savouring it and then going back for more. Deeper this time, just by a fraction. She could do this all day and all night, until they both reached their limits.

'I really don't want to stop...'

'But you think we should?' She knew that he was offering her a way out. If they went back now, then they could both pretend nothing had happened. No harm done.

'I think that... I think it's going to compromise both of us if we take this where I want it to go.' He wound a few strands of her hair around his finger with an expression of regret. He was good at this. He knew exactly how to let a woman down gently. Cori found herself wondering how many times he'd done this before.

The *how many times* made her hesitate just a moment too long. Suddenly his hands were on her shoulders and he had her at arm's length. 'You know, what I really want is to spend some time with you. Just to talk.'

Despite her raging want for him, this was the most thrilling thing of all. His scent might make her feel giddy, his touch might send shivers through her body, but this was something different. Hadn't Jean always told her, in those difficult teenage years, that finding someone to sleep with was easy enough, but finding someone to talk to was a lot harder?

And Dr Tom Riley, the man with the reputation, wanted to talk to her.

Perhaps Rosie had exaggerated things, but Cori somehow doubted it. 'Talking would be...something different.'

His eyes narrowed as he scanned her face. 'So you heard? I'm told I have something of a reputation.'

Tom was obviously expecting her to say that she'd heard nothing of the sort, because his eyebrows shot up when Cori nodded.

'Who...?'

'I'm definitely not going to tell you that.'

'No. That's probably for the best.' His sigh was perhaps a bit too theatrical and clearly for her benefit. 'Things were a lot easier before I took on this job.'

'I think you make a very good head of paediatrics.'

'*Acting* head...' He slicked his hand back through his hair in a gesture of frustration. 'Which makes it quite impossible for me to mention that your eyes are beautiful. Even on my day off.'

'They're not beautiful.'

'So what are they, then?'

Cori wasn't sure. A little too noticeable for her face maybe... 'Startling.'

He chuckled. 'I'll give you that. Startlingly beautiful. Although, of course, I shouldn't be saying that. Or probably even thinking it, at least not for another six weeks.'

Was that what he thought? That the only reason they made a potentially explosive and dangerous mix was that he was her boss? What about the volatile mix of a man who didn't play for keeps and a woman who did?

'You know what. You said you wanted to take another look at the paintings. Let's go down to the tea shop and we can have something to eat and talk about your plans for the unit.' Getting out of there before they both gave in to temptation seemed like the way to go.

He gave her a grin that radiated sex and sent blood rushing to her head. 'Good plan. We'll take this relationship to another level, shall we?'

He'd always been so careful. Always made sure that his partners knew that he didn't really do long term. Before long, word had got around and his reputation precluded the need for that awkward conversation. Tom Riley would be good company, a good lover, he'd end it well and never breathe a word about anything after that ending. But the one thing he didn't do was for ever.

He wasn't proud of that. For ever was something that he'd seen most of his friends embark on, and each time he'd wished he could do that himself. But surviving his father's emotional and physical violence hadn't come without a cost. Tom had shut it all out and learned to make a life for himself, and now opening himself up to anyone seemed an impossible risk.

'So which ones are yours?' He tucked those thoughts away, out of sight, where they belonged.

'Hmm. I don't think I'm going to tell you.' She flashed him a smile over her tea cup. 'You might feel the urge to be nice.'

'I don't *have* to be nice. It's my day off, remember. No rules.' Cori always made him feel as if there weren't any rules. He'd almost disregarded all his personal and professional rules and blundered into something… He didn't need to think about that either. They'd brushed against the point of no return and then drawn back. And the rules mentioned absolutely nothing about enjoying someone's company.

'I'm not telling you, all the same.'

'A test, then.' He grinned at her. 'To see if I can pick yours out as the best, without having known that they were yours.'

She flushed a little, confirming his suspicions. 'I don't expect you to do that.'

'You'd like me to, though.'

'I'm an artist. Of course I'd *like* you to. But I'd appreciate your honest opinion.'

'Okay.' He leaned back in his chair, aware that Cori was sitting bolt upright, her fingers clutching her cup tightly. 'Well, this is going to be tricky.'

He picked a seascape, which he was pretty sure wasn't Cori's but that he liked anyway. He was sure the vase of flowers, a cascade of blues and purples with a twist of individuality, had to be hers, but she shook her head, grinning.

'That's Marianne's. We were at art school together.'

'Close but no cigar, then.' His gaze ranged over the wall. The intricate pencil rendering of a London skyline wasn't hers, neither was the abstract. Cori was far too involved with people. He rather hoped that the dark rendering of a crowded, rain-soaked street at night wasn't hers either. There was something disturbing about it, although Tom couldn't quite work out what.

'What are you thinking?' She was looking at him intently, and Tom realised that he'd been staring at the painting.

'I'm…' He was suddenly at a loss for words. 'That one's…challenging.'

'Yeah? Challenging how?'

'I don't know. I'm no expert on art.'

She grinned. 'But you know what you like. Everyone knows what they like.'

'I suppose so. It's not that I don't *like* it, I just couldn't live with it.' Tom studied the picture carefully, trying to work out exactly how he felt about the painting. The figures on the street seemed so alone, hunched over and hurrying to escape the rain. 'I can't quite get to grips with it…'

He turned as Cori snorted with laughter.

'I've put my foot in my mouth, haven't I? It's yours.'

'Yep. It's mine.'

He should have known. He couldn't take his eyes off the picture, and he didn't know what to make of it. Who else could have painted it but Cori? 'Sorry. I didn't mean…'

'Don't be silly. I love that it makes you feel something.' She looked over at the painting. 'It's called *Walking Home Alone*. It's about isolation, in a crowd.'

Tom looked again. The more he looked, the more it seemed to be speaking just to him. It was almost an effort not to stand up, walk over to it and touch it.

'When you painted it… It seems very personal. Is it something you know about?'

She nodded, looking at him thoughtfully. 'I think we all do in one way or another. When I was a kid I used to feel I was the only one in the world who didn't have a family. I was quite wrong, of course.'

'And then you were adopted.'

'Yes. Then I went to Ralph and Jean. Best thing that ever happened to me.'

Tom nodded. Cori may have found her way out of the loneliness that the painting portrayed so starkly, but he'd never quite shaken the feeling. It was the loneliness of having a secret. Keeping it, until it became so much a part of you that you couldn't let go.

'That one's mine too.' She seemed to sense that he'd

had enough of this guessing game and pointed to another painting, this one of children playing on a beach.

'That one I like.' It was warm, uncomplicated and portrayed the kind of childhood everyone should have.

'Yeah. I painted it to be liked.'

'Not the other one?'

She smiled. 'Not particularly. I like that you picked it out, though.'

He'd done something right, even if he wasn't quite sure what. And he'd made Cori smile, which was fast becoming the one and only object of his afternoon.

CHAPTER SEVEN

CORI WAS WORKING harder than she had ever done in her life. Together, she and Tom were exploring the things that she could do in eight weeks, rather than the things she couldn't. There was a whole unit full of children with different medical conditions and different needs, and only a few short weeks remaining to leave something lasting behind.

The whole unit had been invited to come up with fundraising ideas, and suggestions came flooding in. It became apparent that Tom had been doing some serious promotion of the gallery at the tea shop, and the artists' group couldn't supply enough canvases to keep the wall completely full. She suspected that Tom had purchased a painting too, and noticed that *Walking Home Alone* had been sold, for cash, to an unknown buyer. At this rate they were going to have enough money to provide murals for the whole hospital, but Tom had jealously chased away any other heads of department who'd had the temerity to try and divert Cori from her work in the paediatric unit.

If only this could last. She made the most of every moment, knowing that this was the job she wanted more than anything, and consoling herself with the thought that when her eight weeks were up she could always return to help out on a voluntary basis with some of the projects she was starting.

* * *

Tom's alarm had gone off an hour early and he lay in bed, wondering why. He had a horrible feeling that there was somewhere he'd promised to be.

His phone rang and he answered without looking at the caller display. It had to be the hospital at this time in the morning. 'Tom Riley.'

'What are you wearing?'

'Cori?' His hand slid over his chest. If she really wanted to know what he wore in bed, she could come over and find out…

'If it's not running gear, you'd better hurry up. I'm just about to get into my car so I'll be with you in twenty minutes.'

Right. He remembered now. There was nothing like an early-morning wake-up call to remind him why he usually ran in the evening after work.

When Cori arrived, clad in leggings and a fleece jacket, the day brightened considerably. It was only a short way to the park, and Tom began to feel the familiar surge of strength in his body as it warmed up, ready to take on a little more speed.

'How far is it around the perimeter?' She stopped at the park gates to stretch a little, and Tom followed suit, trying to keep his mind off the slim curve of her hips.

'About twice as far as we'll have to run for the challenge. I reckon we take it slowly until we get to the half-way mark, then see what we can do.'

'Okay. I'm a little nervous about this. I only run three times a week and I don't know if I can go at the pace we need.'

'We'll see what our time is first. Then we can worry about whether we can do it or not.' Tom knew that he had the speed, and if it was humanly possible to get Cori around the course, he'd do it.

The idea was simple enough. Five teams of runners would complete a relay through the streets of central London. The twist to it was that the runners weren't racing against time, or each other, but against five teams who were travelling by public transport, using their wits to find the quickest route on the day.

It was possible. Buses and trains covered the distance much faster, but over short stretches the runners had the advantage of not having to wait for traffic or the next train. The idea had already caught everyone's imagination. They'd had little trouble finding enough people to make up all the teams, and the 'Runners' and 'Riders' were already busy planning the quickest routes between the handover points.

They finished their warm-up and started to run. Cori had a sweet style. Graceful and economical, she seemed to float along, easily keeping up with Tom on the first half of their circuit.

'Ready to speed up?' He shot a grin at her as they approached the halfway mark.

'Yes. Go for it.'

She seemed to be handling their present pace pretty well, and the exhilaration of running with her egged him on to speed up, perhaps a little more than he should. But she responded, and Tom felt a rush of pleasure. This was going to be a lot more fun than he'd bargained for.

Tom began to push a little, and Cori lengthened her stride, seeing his nod when she didn't fall back. When they were close to the end of the circuit he pushed it up another gear, his strong frame making mincemeat of the now punishing pace.

She was falling behind. Cori fixed her eyes on his back

and concentrated on closing the space between them. She made a little headway and saw him glance behind.

Keep going. She willed him not to slow down, digging deep for just a little extra speed. She wanted to show him that she could do it.

'Come on…' His shouted words of encouragement spurred her on, and she put her head down and sprinted. As they reached the gates of the park she drew level with him.

'Nice.' There was real approval in his tone, even though Cori was gasping for air and he seemed hardly out of breath.

'Time…' She managed to get out just the one word.

He consulted the stopwatch strapped to his wrist. 'We're pretty much on target already. If we keep training, we'll do it without any problem at all. I reckon two fast-paced runs for a couple of weeks, and then step it up to three.'

'Two…' She gave up the unequal struggle and just nodded to indicate that she was up for that.

He waited for her to recover and then fell in step with her as she began to jog through the park gates and onto the pavement at a gentle speed. She felt exhilarated beyond the expected endorphin effect. She'd kept up with Tom and earned his respect.

And running beside him made her feel good. He felt strong and dependable, and he was able to set a pace and keep to it. It was even permissible to admire his body, under the guise of assessing his muscle tone.

'I'll see you at work in…an hour?' Tom stopped by her car, looking at his watch.

'Yes. Thanks for this morning. I really enjoyed it.'

He nodded, bending to brush his lips against her cheek. It was the very briefest of encounters, but it took Cori's breath away. He turned, without waiting for any response from her, and walked away quickly.

* * *

The text was ordinary enough—when she had a moment, could Cori come to Tom's office? But when she got there she wished she hadn't waited the twenty minutes until the children in her charge were ready to go for lunch. Tom looked dreadful, pale and haggard, as if he might be bleeding to death from some concealed wound.

'What's wrong?'

'Nothing.' He avoided her gaze. 'I just wondered if you could help with a patient.'

'Of course.' Cori sat down quickly in the chair opposite his desk. Something *was* bothering Tom and she didn't want to leave until she found out what.

'I… We have a new patient in Bay Six. Seven-year-old boy, with newly diagnosed diabetes. He's going to be here for a couple of weeks while we stabilise him.'

'Okay. And I can help with that?'

Tom shook his head. 'No, we've got that covered. I want you to see if you can get him to talk.'

'About what?'

'He has a lot of bruises.' Tom's gaze dropped to the surface of the desk in front of him.

'And that's not due to the diabetes?'

'Increased susceptibility to bruising and slow healing *are* a symptom of diabetes. I want to make sure that's all it is, though, and I'd like you to work with him.'

Cori caught her breath. Tom must think that it was serious or he wouldn't have even suggested this. 'You have concerns about him?'

'I have.' He shook his head. The blankness in his eyes was beginning to frighten Cori. 'I have a feeling. That's all. I've spoken to the hospital's social worker and we've agreed that I'll try to find out more from him over the next few days.'

'And you want me to talk with him.'

'Yeah. Or paint…or whatever. Whatever you need to do to find out whether there's any need for further action on our part.'

'Okay. You've spoken to him?'

'No.'

Something prickled at the back of Cori's neck. The very same instinct that Tom was experiencing with the boy perhaps. Something was wrong and she couldn't put her finger on what it was.

'Is there a reason why you haven't spoken with him yet?'

'Cori, can you just do it?' His tone was level, but his hand was shaking. Tom gripped the arm of his chair in an obvious attempt to steady the tremors, and seemed to take a deep breath. 'I'm sorry. I didn't mean to snap. Today's turning into a bad day.'

'That's okay. I wish you would.'

'Would what?'

'Snap. I wish you'd snap.'

He smiled at her. That luminous, melting smile that reached all of the pleasure centres of her brain. It made her blood run cold.

'Don't do that, Tom.'

'Do what?' He spread his hands in a gesture of innocence.

'Stop pretending that there's nothing going on.' The illusion of a man who was untroubled was so perfect that Cori almost began to doubt herself. But it was too perfect. Somewhere, locked behind the barrier of Tom's impenetrable good humour, there was a wounded soul, screaming to be heard.

'There *is* nothing going on.' He was regarding her steadily.

'Okay.' She got to her feet. She had to move before she started raging at him, and Cori's instinct was that her rage would only make him retreat even more. 'I'll go and see the boy this afternoon. I'll let you know what my thoughts are.'

'Thank you. I'd appreciate that.'

That look. The one that said nothing was the matter and betrayed just a trace of relief that she was going along with the lie. She couldn't bear it. Planting her hands on his desk, she leaned across until they were face to face.

'We're not done yet, Tom.'

Turning quickly, before he could come out with any more denials, she walked out of his office.

Tom wondered whether she was aware he was watching her, and came to the conclusion that she must know. But Cori didn't seem to mind, and it settled Tom's raging emotions to do so.

He'd seen children who had been abused before, far too many of them. And although every mark inflicted on a child's skin was unacceptable, he'd seen cases that were a lot worse than this one. So why now?

Because of Cori maybe. He watched as she smiled at Jamie, sitting down by his bedside. She didn't push the paper at him but did quite the reverse, putting the brightly coloured pencils and the paper just out of his reach, as if it was a coincidence that she had them with her. When Jamie reached for them himself, she slid them a little closer, smiling in that impish way she had.

If he'd had someone like Cori when he'd been a kid... Tom had thought about that prospect more than once. Someone who might have come to his rescue when he was still young, before all the hang-ups had become an inseparable part of him, as if they were set in stone.

Suddenly, in his imagination, he was Jamie's age again, sitting in the warmth of Cori's smile. Right away he knew that wasn't really what he wanted. In the imaginary world where anyone could be any age they liked, he narrowed the age gap between them and imagined her at six years old and himself at eight. *He* would be protecting *her*, holding her hand and being her friend. And that, somehow, would heal his own pain.

'Tom!' Someone spoke insistently behind him and he jumped.

'Yeah, sorry.' He turned away from Cori and the image dissolved, taking a little bit of his heart with it.

Kate, the senior nurse on duty, handed him the notes for the child in the bed across from Jamie's. 'Do you need anything else?' Her querying look reminded Tom that a visit to this particular bay wasn't on his schedule for the day.

'No, it's fine. Thanks, Kate, I'm just checking up on something.' He focused his eyes on the notes in front of him and then handed them back. 'Fine. That's fine. Thanks very much.' Tom strode out of the ward, leaving Jamie in Cori's care.

He was almost disappointed to find that his car was just as he'd left it. No fairies on the windscreen, no folded dinosaurs under the wipers. Tom wondered whether she would have left something, just a sprinkle of glitter maybe, if Cori had known how he felt right now.

His hand shook as he reached into his pocket and his keys slipped through his fingers and fell to the concrete. He wanted to forget about all that had happened today and just talk with Cori. Just be with her and feel her warmth.

He let the phone ring three times and then hung up. Cori wasn't answering. It was suddenly calming to know that he was alone. If he was alone then he couldn't hurt or be hurt.

He took a deep breath, picked up his keys from the ground and disengaged the locks on the car doors. Automatically, he went through the motions. Opening the back door to throw his briefcase and coat onto the seat. Getting behind the steering wheel. He was in control now. It had been stupid to think that he needed anyone else.

His phone rang, and he jumped. When he looked at the caller display he almost didn't answer. Then he heard Cori's voice on the other end of the line, almost as if someone else had answered for him.

'Tom… Are you there?'

'Yeah, sorry. I must have pocket-dialled you.'

'Okay.'

From the tone of her voice she didn't buy that for a moment.

'Look, I've just walked in through my front door. Would you like to come over?'

'What for?' He knew exactly what for. This was an invitation to explain himself.

'Nothing in particular. Just pop in if you feel like it. I've learned how to make hot chocolate. Once I got to grips with the coffee, I felt I wanted to branch out a bit. It's pretty good.'

'That would be great. But can I take a rain check? I've got something to do tonight. Another time.'

'Of course.'

There was a pause, as if something else needed to be said but neither of them was going to make the first move.

'Look after yourself, Tom.'

'Yeah. See you.'

He always *had* looked after himself, there had never been anyone else that he could depend on. He'd grown up and become strong enough to defend himself. No one could touch him now, not even Cori.

CHAPTER EIGHT

CORI WAS TWIRLING her brush thoughtfully in a dab of scarlet paint, wondering whether a red slash of colour on the canvas was what she really wanted to do, when the doorbell rang. Dinner was served.

She hurried through the hallway and threw open the main door. Tom was standing on the doorstep, under a large umbrella.

'Oh.' The brush slipped from her fingers and clattered onto the floor. 'You're not my pizza.'

'No, I'm not.' He bent to pick up the brush and handed it to her. 'Is that a problem?'

'No. I just wasn't expecting you.'

'I came to…' Tom clearly had no more of an idea than she did about what he was doing there. But when she looked up into his face, she thought she saw pain.

'Whatever it is, you can't do it on the doorstep. Come in.'

He gave a small nod, folding down the umbrella and giving it a shake, before propping it in the porch. Each one of his movements was sparing and controlled, and it seemed like he was trying to keep it all together.

He sat down wearily on the sofa, as if he'd come a long way to get here. Cori sat down silently next to him. Whatever happened next, it had to come from him.

'I should apologise. I…' He shrugged, seemingly lost for words.

'You have nothing to apologise for. You seem to have something on your mind, and I'd really like to help, if I can.'

Her doorbell rang. Damn, this wasn't the time.

'Your bell…'

'I know. It's my pizza. Forget it.'

'Aren't you hungry?' A twitch at the corner of Tom's mouth said that he knew that he'd quite literally been saved by the bell. That he'd got himself in too deep and he was looking for a way to retreat gracefully.

She wasn't going to help him with that. 'Yes. But I want to hear what you've got to say more than I want to eat.' The bell rang again, this time more insistently.

'This can wait. And he'll only keep ringing…'

Cori frowned. Tom was right, you couldn't just leave a pizza delivery guy standing on the doorstep. He'd press the doorbell for every flat in the building. 'Okay. Stay there.'

She ran to the door, flung it open, snatched her pizza and pressed the money for it into the young man's hand. Slamming the door in his face, before he could thank her for the generous tip, she threw the pizza box onto the kitchen counter and sat back down on the sofa, next to Tom. The whole operation took about forty-five seconds.

'Don't you want to put that in the oven?' Tom's demons were making a last-ditch attempt to preserve their hold on him.

'I'd prefer to talk about whatever it was that brought you here in the first place.'

'You promised me hot chocolate.' That smile. The one that seemed so open and inviting and yet hid so much.

'Later. It's too early for that.'

'That's not what you said on the phone.' His tone was

suddenly flirtatious. That was Tom's answer to everything that came a little too close for comfort.

'I thought it went without saying that you'd like a progress report on Jamie first…' Cori gave him the sweetest smile she could, in the face of his blistering, thousand-watt gaze.

He flopped back onto the sofa cushions, grinning. 'All right. Yes, of course I'd like a progress report.'

Cori swallowed hard. If she'd thought that talking about work was going to make things any easier then she'd been wrong. The sizzle between them retreated a little, but not far enough to allow her to think with any clarity.

'We spent a couple of hours together—he seemed to enjoy it and we talked quite a bit. He said nothing about the bruises and I didn't ask.'

'What about his drawings? I saw that you gave him crayons…' Tom was thoughtful now, staring at the ceiling.

'He's been ill, he's in a strange place, and there are obviously some things on his mind. I'm waiting for him to tell me.'

'Do you have any guesses?' Tom turned his head, and his gaze hit her like a bolt of lightning. These were the moments when he was so irresistible. It was the way she'd first seen him, a concerned and committed doctor, who had no reason to hide his passion. As a man, a lover, Tom Riley seemed always to be hiding from something.

'My guess is that this is a process I can't rush. He'll tell me when he's ready.' Cori supposed that Tom would do that too. Only the years had given him a better defence strategy than Jamie was likely to have.

Tom nodded thoughtfully. 'You have a way with the children. They trust you.'

'Thank you…' There was something about Tom's praise that made her crave more, and he seemed to know it.

'You're kind and creative. You know how to weave a spell...' He leaned in a little closer, his gaze mesmerising her. 'A little pushy at times, but I'm getting to like that too. And you have gorgeous eyes.'

Her breath caught, almost choking her. 'Tom, I...'

Maybe her confusion was showing on her face. He seemed to sense it. 'Am I embarrassing you?'

'Well, yes. A little.'

'I just like to pay you compliments. I think you deserve them. But I could stop now, if it makes you uncomfortable.'

She couldn't help smiling. 'Yes. I think you should.'

He nodded. 'Would it be all right if I mentioned that you fold a very mean dinosaur?'

'What are you doing here, Tom?'

'I wanted some company.'

'Why me?'

'Only you would do.' He smiled. That we-know-a-secret smile that rocked her world. 'Can I cook for you?'

'Cook for me?'

'Yeah. I'm a really good cook. Didn't I tell you that?'

'You might have mentioned it. I'm not sure that I entirely believed you, I thought you might be bragging. And there's a perfectly good pizza there that we could heat up.'

He rolled his eyes. 'That pizza's going to be as hard as a brick by now. I can pop to the deli around the corner and get us something better to eat. Don't you want to find out if I'm as good as I say I am?'

'Ohhh!' He was good. Very good.

'You like that?'

'Oh, yes.' Cori felt as if she was melting. 'Again.'

'Wait...wait.' He chuckled quietly. 'Anticipation's the key.'

'You're going to kill me.' Tom's first course had been

delicious, melt-in-the-mouth pasta with a seafood sauce. She'd challenged him to surprise her with the second course, and he'd risen to that challenge.

'No, I'm not.' He let the spoon brush her lips, leaving a smear of molten chocolate, then withdrew it. 'Keep your eyes closed.'

She heard the spoon scrape in the bowl and then felt it touch her tongue, cold this time. 'Mmm. Sorbet. Vanilla sorbet. With something else.'

'Lime.'

'Uh. Nice.'

He let the cold spoon linger against her lips, just a few moments longer than he really needed to. This felt just like sex. It had taken the same kind of trust, closing her eyes and letting him feed her. And she was rapidly getting very turned on.

'Try this.'

She felt the spoon at her lips again, warm this time. She could smell the chocolate. Cori had never stopped to smell chocolate before, but this... He let her have the whole spoonful.

'More?'

'Not yet.' She wanted to savour each note of the bitter-sweet taste in her mouth.

'Now you're getting the idea. Did you know you have hundreds of thousands of taste receptors in your mouth? Different tastes trigger responses at different times, which means that good food is always worth taking your time over.'

She could think about the science later. Right now, all she knew was that each one of those receptors was on high alert and begging for more. If any other guy had tried this, he would have found himself kicked out and unable to walk without pain for a week. But Tom wasn't any other guy, and she'd let him do it. In return he seemed to be doing his best to drive her totally mad with pleasure.

'Here.' He picked up her hand, running her finger around the cool bowl of a drinking glass. There was a sweet fruity smell as he raised the glass to her lips. 'Take a sip.'

'Mmm. That's really nice. Dessert wine... Hey, what are you doing? Are you drinking it too?'

'Just a mouthful. I'm enjoying it with you.' Cori felt the glass against her lips again and took a little of the wine, wondering whether he'd allowed her to drink from the place where his lips had touched the rim. The thought made her head reel.

'I concede. You were right and I was wrong. Food's a sensual experience.' She wondered whether the admission was going to call a halt to this. She hoped not.

'Now I've won you round to my point of view...'

A sweet, unmistakable smell made her smile. 'Mmm. Strawberries...'

Tom woke up with a start. The sensation that Cori was in his arms was still so real that for a moment he thought she was. He rolled over, burying his face in his hands. What on earth had happened last night?

It had all started when Cori had thrown down a challenge. She'd said that creating a desert to die for in half an hour was impossible, and he'd shown her differently. Then she'd shared her own passion with him as they'd sat together in front of a blank canvas. Slowly his own face had emerged, half smiling back at him. As she'd worked, he'd felt her body relax against his, drawing him into her own world of happiness.

He couldn't remember when he'd had a better evening,

or ever having been so loath to say goodnight. But sex with Cori...

His body reacted to the thought, and Tom rolled out of bed, hoping that the chill air might go some way towards dampening his ardour. Being her boss might be a good enough excuse for the next month or so, but sleeping with Cori would be breaking the rules on a far deeper level than that and at some point he was going to have to face up to the real reason. They weren't two friends, sharing something special, on the explicit understanding that it wasn't permanent. If she took him into her bed she'd make him her lover and Tom doubted if he'd walk away from Cori in one piece.

He switched the shower on, shivering at the touch of the cool water. Maybe he should paint her a picture, one that would tell her everything she needed to know about him.

No. Not that. Maybe a letter. Perhaps he should just write down all the things he couldn't say, and then she'd see that he wasn't the man for her. The idea grew in his head, blossoming as the water grew warmer. It was one way to salvage their friendship before he did anything stupid.

CHAPTER NINE

THE NEXT FEW days should have been perfect. Tom was supportive at work, and his creative approach to bureaucracy meant that there were no obstacles to the plans for making the art room into an environment that children would love long after Cori was gone. On Friday evening, a staff meeting in the pub to exchange ideas for fundraising had been well attended and had gone on until closing time.

She told herself that this was all she wanted. Even if Rosie's assessment of Tom wasn't necessarily to be trusted, he hadn't denied it. He was a great boss, a good friend and that should be enough. Cori wasn't in the market for a fling, particularly one that she suspected might just break her heart.

When her phone rang on Saturday morning, she turned over in bed, keeping her eyes firmly closed. Whatever time it was, it was too early.

The phone stopped and started again. Whoever it was wasn't taking no for an answer. She grabbed the handset from the nightstand and held it to her ear.

'What?'

'Still in bed?' Tom's voice came down the line.

'Yes.'

'Then I suppose I shouldn't really ask what you're wearing.'

'You can if you want. I'm not ashamed of being caught wearing pyjamas. Why are you calling?' If he told her that he'd woken her up for an early morning chat, she was going to find and throttle him.

'You asked me to. Call me in the morning, you said, or I'll never make it into work.'

'Okay, you called me. Thanks, Tom.' She cut the line and sank back into the pillows.

The phone rang again.

'Tom!'

'Yeah. You didn't sound really committed about the getting-out-of-bed thing.'

'I'm not.'

'It's just that you said that you wanted to pop in to see Jamie and a couple of the other kids today, and that you had things to do this afternoon, so you needed to get an early start.'

'Uh.' Cori was beginning to remember. She *had* got a busy day today, and she had asked Tom to call her. 'Sorry, I...'

'No matter.'

The doorbell rang. Cori dragged herself out of bed, and somehow managed to get her arms into her dressing gown, while still holding the phone. 'Where are you now?'

'On my way to the hospital.'

'Okay. I'll see who it is at the door, and I'll be on my way in about ten minutes.'

'No, you won't...'

'Why?'

'I've just left breakfast on your front doorstep. Don't hurry it.'

Cori scrambled to the front door and found that Tom had already gone. There was, however, a cardboard box, which on inspection proved to contain hot coffee, warm croissants and a chilled fresh fruit salad.

An hour after he had left breakfast on her doorstep, and then raced back to his car and driven off, Cori walked into the paediatric unit. Tom was sitting in the reception area, looking through the plans for the mural that was to be painted there and trying not to let it appear that he was waiting for her.

She was obviously going somewhere this afternoon, and she looked fabulous in slim-fitting jeans and ankle boots that made her legs look impossibly long. A red knitted jacket, with a matching, multi-coloured scarf slung across her shoulders, accentuated her dark hair and the porcelain of her skin.

'Thank you for breakfast.' A slightly brighter shade of lipstick than usual made her lips look impossibly kissable. The fact that she bent down to deliver the words directly into his ear was rather more than Tom had bargained for.

'You're welcome. I would have come and cooked something, but I decided that would probably constitute housebreaking.'

'Maybe. I wouldn't have reported you, particularly if you were making me breakfast.'

'In that case, I might give it a try.' Tom got to his feet, gathering up his pile of notes. 'Are you ready to see Jamie?'

'Yes, I'll spend some time with him, and then there are a couple of other things I need to do.' She reached into her large leather handbag and pulled out a rag doll. 'Do you think Molly will like this?'

'I think she'll love it.' The doll had red hair like Molly's and freckles. It also had a small lump under its pretty green summer dress, and when Tom investigated a little further he found that it was a replica of Molly's insulin pump.

'I'll leave it on her bed while she's having her lunch.'

Tom had noticed that one of Cori's favourite things was leaving little presents for the children to find. If she could, she'd hide nearby to see their excitement, but if not she'd simply walk away, grinning. He was beginning to see the appeal. If he hadn't seen Cori get such pleasure out of it, he would never have thought to leave breakfast on her doorstep and just drive away.

They walked together to Bay Six, but Jamie wasn't in his bed. A quick check of the toilets and then the art room became a slightly more comprehensive search of anywhere that Jamie might be.

Kate was the senior nurse on duty today, and was the first to be told. 'When did anyone last see him?' Cori could hear the concern in Tom's voice.

'About half an hour ago.'

'That's something. I've been in the reception area for the last three quarters of an hour and it's unlikely he could have slipped past me and out of the unit.'

'All the same, can't be too careful…' Kate's voice was thick with worry. Something like this was potentially one of the unit's worst nightmares, and no one wanted it to happen on their watch.

'Yeah, you're right. I'll call Hospital Security, and get them to review the CCTV tapes opposite the entrance door and check outside for any open doors or windows.' Tom thought hard, remembering the procedure to be followed in the event of a missing child. 'Kate, we'll need six members of staff, to split up into pairs and search the three sections of the unit. We'll do an initial search, and then contact the child protection nurse and the patient services co-ordinator. I'll stay here and I want everyone to report back to me after ten minutes.'

'Got it.' Kate hurried away.

'What can I do?' Cori was at his elbow still, frowning, and Tom remembered that he had resolved not to make the mistake of excluding her again.

'Come with me.'

Tom had taken up his position at the nurses' station so that he could co-ordinate all the people searching for Jamie. He sat down, motioning for Cori to sit with him. 'Okay, so we've covered the systematic approach. What can we add to that?'

Cori thought hard. 'Well, we've already checked the places we'd expect to find him.' She reached into her handbag, pulling out her tablet computer, relieved that she'd brought it with her that morning. 'I've got all of his paintings scanned in. Let's take a look.'

She switched the tablet on, and flipped through the pictures that she'd scanned after each session with Jamie. Stopping at one, she heard Tom's sharp intake of breath behind her.

'I asked Jamie to tell me about this picture, and he said that the figure was him. These heavy lines, almost obscuring him, can be indicative of a desire to hide.' She looked up at Tom, who was staring at the screen. 'You recognise this?'

'I... I don't know. Maybe.' He shook his head. 'This isn't about me, Cori.'

'It's about both of us, using our instinct and imagination to work out where he might go. If you have something to bring to this, then you should do it.'

He didn't reply. She flipped through the pictures slowly, and was almost at the end before he stopped her again. 'Look, he's afraid of something and he thinks you'll protect him.'

'What makes you say that?' Cori had already seen Jamie's fears, a monster with large teeth in the corner of the picture, but she hadn't picked up on her own presence there.

'See there. That sunflower with the smiley face and the beautiful eyes.'

'Oh. You think that's me?' The face had red lips and bright purple eyes.

'Can't you see the resemblance?'

'No, not really...' Cori studied the picture carefully. 'These all give some indication of his general state of mind, but there's nothing that tells us where he might be.'

'Okay, so look at it another way. What's his general state of mind?' Tom's brow was furrowed in thought.

'He generally seems quite a happy little boy, but there is something bothering him. Something that frightens him.'

'So he might be hiding?'

'Maybe. Where would *you* hide if you wanted to keep out of everyone's way?'

Tom shrugged. 'I'm a bit bigger than Jamie. The only place I can find to hide around here is my office.'

'Hmm. Has anyone actually checked your office?'

'I don't know. Jamie doesn't even know where it is, does he?'

'Of course he does. His bed is by the entrance to the bay, and there's a glazed panel that lets him see all the way up the corridor. He watches you going in and out all the time.' Cori wondered if she'd just betrayed the fact that *she* had been watching Tom too from Jamie's bedside.

They stared at each other for a moment. It suddenly seemed the obvious place that Jamie would go.

'Only one way to find out.' Tom was on his feet, striding past Bay Six, where Jamie's empty bed was, towards his office door. When he twisted the door handle, it didn't give.

'Did you lock it, Tom?'

'No, but I left my keys on my desk.' He raised his knuckle to the door to rap on it and then thought better of it. 'I don't really want to frighten him if he is in there.'

He tried to peer through the glazed panel to one side of the door, but the blind between the two panes of glass was closed. Cori saw that the skylight, above the door, was unobscured, and tapped his arm.

'If you can give me a leg up, I'll look through there.'

She took off her boots, expecting him to lace his fingers together and boost her up the two feet she needed to peer through the skylight. Instead, he lifted her bodily upwards, and she clung to his shoulders for balance.

'You're a lot stronger than I thought...' She gripped hold of the edge of the skylight to pull herself up a little higher.

'Yeah. You're a lot heavier than I thought...'

'Thanks!'

'What? I thought fairies didn't weigh any more than a mustard seed. What can you see?'

'Hang on...' Cori peered through the glass and then she saw him. Jamie was sitting in Tom's high-backed chair, staring solemnly at her. Cori grinned, waving at him. 'Hi, Jamie...'

'He's there?'

'Yep.' Cori gave the boy an encouraging smile. 'Sweetie, can you unlock the door?'

Jamie shook his head.

'What's he doing?' Tom's hand had strayed to her bottom, but since she felt much steadier that way, Cori decided not to protest. Needs must.

'He's just sitting there, grinning at me. And it doesn't look as if he's going to open the door.'

'How does he look? Is he drowsy?'

'I'm no doctor, but he looks absolutely fine to me.'

'Ask him to unlock the door again. I don't want to

frighten him by having to break down the door... Kate...'
The nurse appeared at the other end of the corridor and he
called to her. 'He's in here. Will you let everyone know
they can stop looking for him now?'

Cori made a few funny faces at Jamie and he made a
few back. Then she asked him again to open the door and
he shook his head. 'He isn't going to do it. Let me down
for a minute.'

She felt herself sliding down his body, and tried not to
think about it. He set her down onto her feet, the trace of
a smile on his lips.

'Perhaps I can pick the lock.'

Tom's eyes widened. 'You know how to pick a lock?'

'You learn a lot of very handy things in a children's
home.' Cori picked up her handbag, searching for something that might do the job, and felt her fingers scrape
against an old nail file.

Kneeling down, she peered into the lock. 'The key's in
there, but I think...' A sharp, well-placed jab with the nail
file meant the key fell out of the lock on the other side.
'Just as well he doesn't know the old trick of turning the
key a quarter turn.'

She heard Tom's chair creak, and light footsteps running to the other side of the door. Jamie's eye appeared,
looking through the keyhole at her. 'Hi, Jamie. Go and sit
down, sweetie.'

Cori straightened up. 'He obviously reckons this is some
kind of game, I can hear him laughing. We'll have to get
him away from the door. I'm not jabbing a nail file into
the lock if he's on the other side of it. And you can't break
the door down either.'

Tom's brow furrowed in thought. 'We'll just have to
reason with him. Wait there.' He strode to the end of the
corridor where a small group had gathered to see what was

happening. Sending one off in one direction, and following another the opposite way, he reappeared a few moments later, carrying a small stepladder.

He planted it on the floor outside the door and climbed the three steps to the top. 'Hey, Jamie...' Cori heard the boy scamper away from the door, so that he could see Tom. 'I've given the nurses the slip and come to rescue you.'

It was an approach. And from the muffled sounds of Jamie's greeting through the door, it was working. 'Jamie... Jamie, you need to take cover while we get the door open. There might be a bit of an explosion, so hide under the desk.'

'Oh, please...' Cori heard Kate behind her, muttering under her breath. 'They never grow up, do they?'

Cori chuckled, and turned to see her holding a crowbar. 'Here.' She handed it up to Tom.

'Ah, you've got it, thanks.' He turned to look through the skylight again. 'That's right, Jamie. Right underneath. That's it, mate. Now stay there until I tell you to come out.'

'I could try the lock, now that he's away from the door...' Cori volunteered. 'Might take a little while.'

'Let's play it safe and get him out of there now.' Tom stepped down from the ladder and fitted the crowbar between the door and the jamb. 'Keep an eye on him, make sure he stays put, will you?'

Cori took his place on the ladder, peering through the skylight. 'Okay. He's under your desk, and he's got his hands over his ears.'

'Yeah...' Tom twisted the crowbar in a short, sharp movement. There was a crack and the door drifted open a couple of inches. He handed the crowbar back to Kate, and then made a show of stumbling into the room, almost collapsing onto the floor.

Kate let out a sigh, shaking her head. 'And I have to

work around all this...' She was grinning, though, obviously as pleased with the creative approach to problem-solving as Cori was.

Jamie appeared from under the desk and started to run around, hallooing. Tom herded him behind the desk and lifted him up into his chair. 'Okay, mate. Let's have a look at you, and make sure you're all right. That was pretty exciting, wasn't it?'

'You banged down the door...' Jamie was clearly impressed with Tom's efforts.

'Yes, that's right.' Tom picked up his keys from the floor and pocketed them, bending down in front of Jamie. 'Sit still for a minute.'

He quickly examined Jamie, nodding towards Kate. 'Okay, he's all right. Perhaps we could get him a drink. Would you like something to drink, Jamie?'

Jamie nodded. 'I want to stay here.'

'Well, I've got some things to do, so maybe you'll look after things here while I'm gone. Perhaps Cori will sit with you, eh?' Tom's gaze found hers and Cori nodded, smiling at Jamie.

'We'll make dinosaurs, shall we? I've got some paper in my room, I'll just go and get it.'

'Yes-s-s!'

Jamie had finally said it. After days of letting him know that it was okay to say whatever he wanted to her, he'd explained the bruises. Kate was sitting quietly by the door, and exchanged a quick glance and a nod with Cori.

After half an hour Jamie seemed relaxed enough to go back to the ward, and Kate took him away.

'He'll have someone with him?'

The nurse nodded. 'Yes. I'll make sure someone's keeping an eye on him.' She gave Jamie the special smile that all the nurses seemed to reserve for their young patients. 'We'll go and get some lunch, shall we, Jamie? Adventurers all need a good lunch...'

Tom was in the reception area, deep in conversation with one of the junior doctors, and Cori hung back, waiting for him to finish. When he saw her, he shot her a smile. She mouthed that she'd be in the canteen and he nodded, returning to his conversation.

As she walked to the door, a man pushed past her, almost knocking her off her feet. He was tall and burly, with anger seeping from every pore. Cori turned to see if there was anyone to deal with him, and saw him marching towards Tom.

'You... I want a word.'

Everyone in the reception area jumped as his voice rang out.

'Mr Morton—' Tom didn't get a chance to say whatever it was he was about to say to Jamie's father as a woman who had been running in his wake put herself between the two men.

'Jack, don't.' Tears were running down her face and her voice cracked into a pleading tone. 'Please... She told us not to say anything...'

'It's okay.' Everyone else seemed to have shrunk away from the man, but Tom squared up to him. 'Perhaps you'd like to come to my office and we can talk about what's on your mind.'

His reasonable tone seemed to enrage the man even more. He moved his wife out of the way and held his fist in Tom's face.

Tom didn't even flinch. It was as if he was entirely indifferent to whether the man hit him or not, but Mrs Morton started to cry in earnest now. 'No, Jack, you're making things worse…' She turned to Tom. 'He's not like that, he's just angry…'

'Be quiet, Marion, and sit down. This is between him and me.'

That was one thing that the two men seemed to agree on at least. Tom guided Mrs Morton to one side, and Kate led her firmly away. Then he turned back to face Mr Morton.

'Mr Morton, you need to calm down right now.'

'No. *You* need to buck your ideas up a bit. I've had enough of you people. You're supposed to be looking after my son and this morning I find out that you lost him.'

'Jamie was found in my office, no more than fifteen minutes after he went missing. We called you to let you know.'

'Don't think that I don't know what you're up to. I heard about your little plan to take him away from us and you're not going to do it.'

'Mr Morton, there's no plan, we're simply responding to Jamie's needs and to questions that have arisen.' Tom's voice was still calm, still measured, even though he must be asking the same silent questions Cori was. Who had told Jamie's father about their suspicions? Nothing had been made official yet.

'And how would you know what's best for *my* son?' The man was still shouting at the top of his voice. 'Don't think that I don't know where you're coming from. Your father beat you and you think that all fathers are the same. Wake up, mate, because they're not.'

There was a sudden, shocked silence. Cori could almost see the life draining from Tom, leaving just an expression-less husk behind.

'I think we should take this conversation somewhere else.' Tom went to move Jack Morton towards the door.

'What, I'm too near the truth for comfort?'

'No, you're too near a ward full of sick children to be raising your voice like this. We'll take it elsewhere.'

'We'll take it nowhere...' The door of the unit clicked shut and Cori looked around to see two of the hospital's security guards walking towards them. Mr Morton turned and took a swing at Tom.

Tom saw it coming and stepped back, but he couldn't avoid the fist entirely. There was a dull smack and blood started to trickle down Tom's chin.

Then everyone seemed to be moving. One of the security guards took Jack Morton's arm, pulling him away from Tom, and someone produced a paper towel, which he held to his lip. Tom seemed to be trying to calm everyone down.

The guards were hustling Jack Morton out of the unit, no doubt intending to defuse the situation. Tom was about to follow when Cori caught his arm.

'I have to talk to you. Now.'

'Can't it wait?' There was nothing in his eyes. No pain or anger. Just nothing. Was Jack Morton right? Was this the thing that Tom hid so carefully from everyone?

'No, it can't wait. It's about Jamie and it's really important. You need to speak to me before you speak to anyone else.'

'Okay. Later.' Tom signalled to the security guards, and exchanged a few words with them, suggesting that a cup of tea in one of the quiet rooms might give everyone a chance to calm down. The two of them ambled off on either side of Jack Morton, who was visibly regaining his composure.

'Tom...?'

He exchanged a nod with Kate, who was shepherding a sobbing Mrs Morton after her husband. Then he turned abruptly, without a word to anyone, and without even looking in Cori's direction he strode out of the unit.

CHAPTER TEN

HE COULD HEAR her voice behind him, but Tom didn't stop. He didn't know where he was going, he just needed to put some space between himself and everything that had happened this morning.

'Tom! Slow down.'

He increased his pace, walking out of the main doors of the hospital and into the freezing wind. Cori was one of the few people who knew about his concerns for Jamie, and the only one who knew that he had a personal reason for not talking to Jamie himself. She had to have worked it out, and the thought that, while she'd said nothing to him, she must have said something to someone else made Tom want to curl up and disappear.

'Tom...'

He'd thought that he could make good. Thought he could leave his childhood behind him when he'd left home and come to London. He'd made a life for himself, untainted by his father's violence, and now it had come back to smack him in the gut in the very worst way possible. Cori had betrayed him.

'Tom! Face me!' Her tone had turned from supplication to challenge. Tom whirled around, before he quite knew what he was doing.

'What? You think I can't?'

She was jogging to catch up with him, her cheeks pink and her eyes hot with emotion. 'No. I think you can't face how angry you are at being on the end of someone's fist.'

She was wrong. He'd learned to swallow that anger, to push it away. 'No, Cori. What I can't face is someone going behind my back. It's unprofessional.'

Unprofessional, and it hurt like hell. He'd allowed Cori in and she'd got to the very heart of him. Now he was paying the price.

'You think...' Her cheeks flushed deeper now. 'You think it was *me*?'

'I think you spoke to *someone*. Maybe you didn't realise the consequences...'

He'd thought that he was just giving her a way to confess without losing too much face, but fire flared in her eyes and Cori glared up at him.

'Don't patronise me, Tom. I'm perfectly well aware of the consequences of breaking a confidence.' She shot him a meaningful look. 'Even one that's not explicitly a confidence.'

She was right. He'd hinted at the truth but had never told her not to say anything. Maybe on some level he'd wanted her to know. Tom never would have thought she'd use that knowledge for this, though.

'Who else could it be, then? You were the only one who knew...' He broke off and turned away from her. He couldn't do this. Couldn't see the look in her eyes when she finally ran out of excuses and admitted that it had been her.

He took two steps, and then he felt her grab his arm. He could have shaken her off easily, but if he knew Cori at all he knew she'd hang on for all she was worth. It took an effort to calm himself and face her, but somehow he did it.

Her face was determined. 'I won't deny that I put two and two together, and thought that you had some personal experience of violence as a child. And I could probably manage to prove that I didn't talk to the Mortons. But I'm not going to do that, because I'm asking you to just believe me. I didn't speak to anyone, about you or about Jamie.'

'You want me to just take your word for it.' Suddenly that didn't seem so much to ask. And suddenly Tom knew it was what he wanted to do, more than anything.

'Yes, I do. I'm trusting you that you're not going to reject what I say out of hand.'

Then he saw it. The child who had been rejected time and time again had turned into a woman who was brave enough to reach out and demand his acceptance. And she didn't do it lightly. She did it because she knew that she deserved it.

He took a deep breath. 'I'm sorry, Cori. I... I do believe you.' The words weren't as difficult to say as he'd thought.

'Thank you.' The fire in her eyes died suddenly, and one tear rolled down her cheek. *His* tear. Suddenly he knew that it was for him alone, and Tom bent, brushing it away with a kiss, which stung as the salt found the cut on his lip.

'I bet that smarts.' She smiled up at him.

'Yeah. Sorry... Look, you've got a little blood on your cheek.'

She rubbed at her face, never taking her gaze from him. 'That's okay. You've got a little salt in your wound.'

'Yeah. Quite a lot, actually.'

'And it hurts?' She clearly wasn't talking about the cut any more.

'Hurts like hell.' He didn't want to tell her it was okay, or that it was all behind him now and none of it mattered any more. He'd been telling himself that for too long.

She nodded. 'I'm sorry that happened to you.'

He gave a small stiff nod, not wanting to think that this was anything more than just the right thing to say, not daring to imagine that she understood how he was feeling. 'Go inside. You'll catch a cold.'

She'd come out without a coat, and she was shivering now, but she shook her head. 'Come back with me.'

The last thing he wanted was to go back to the unit. Everyone would be talking about what Jack Morton had said, and wondering whether it was true. However much they might understand, however sympathetic they might be, he'd spent the last eighteen years distancing himself from it and he just didn't want to go back there.

'No.'

'Then I'm going with you.'

'Cori, you have no idea where I'm going.'

'Yeah, I do. You're going back to that place where you're humiliated and hurt and you can't escape. Trust me, I know exactly where that is. And you're not going there on your own.'

'Cori...' He turned away from her, and the freezing wind seemed to slap him in the face, making his jaw throb and his cut lip sting. He might not have any idea what he was going to do next, but suddenly it didn't feel as if walking away from Cori would solve anything.

He took off his jacket and tried to wrap it around her shoulders, but she shrugged him away. She had tears in her eyes.

'I'm going to the canteen. Are you coming?' He didn't wait for her answer, and wouldn't let her escape this time when he bundled her into his jacket. He put his arm around her, and hurried her across the courtyard.

At least he'd stopped running. She let him hustle her inside, and through the doors into the warmth of the canteen.

'Tea?' He felt in his pocket and pulled out a handful of

coins. 'I left my wallet in my desk drawer, but I think I've got enough for a buttered bun between us...'

She felt in her jeans pocket and found a pound coin. 'Get two.'

'Okay. Find a table.'

He brought the tray across and unloaded the cups and plates onto the table. Careful and precise, it was as if he had to think about everything he did at the moment.

'What was it you wanted to tell me? About Jamie.'

Maybe he was just trying to change the subject, get onto easier ground. But the situation with Jamie's parents demanded that he hear this sooner rather than later. 'We were making dinosaurs and he was getting one of the models to fight with the other. He said he was going to bash Kevin like that.

Tom raised an eyebrow. 'Kevin?'

'Apparently Kevin is his babysitter's boyfriend. From what I can gather, the babysitter has her boyfriend round when she's alone in the house with Jamie. He gets left to his own devices to get himself washed and into bed. They lock themselves in the living room and if Jamie wants something and bangs on the door, the boyfriend isn't too pleased about it.'

'So it's not the father?'

'I never got that impression, from the way that Jamie talks about his dad.'

'How does he talk about him?' Tom looked puzzled.

'Well, for a start, he talks about him. He told me how he's been building a shed in the garden, and that he lets Jamie help him.' Cori imagined that Tom hadn't mentioned doing anything with his own father in the course of conversation for the last eighteen years.

Tom nodded, the twitch of a pulse showing at his

temple. 'I'm glad it's not his father. But why didn't he tell someone?'

'He was afraid.'

Sadness and pain showed on Tom's face. 'I'd better go. I have to sort this all out...'

'It's okay. They don't need you. Kate was with me and she heard everything.' But Tom was obviously not going to allow Kate to deal with this if he was on the premises, and was already reaching for his coat. 'Why don't you call Kate? It may well be better if you stayed out of the way for a little while.'

Tom didn't look convinced, but he made the call. Whatever Kate had to say seemed to put his mind at rest.

'She's called the duty social worker and they've talked to Mr and Mrs Morton, and reassured them as best they can. They're with Jamie now. It appears I'm surplus to requirements for the moment.'

'Good. Then we can stay here and talk. About what happened to you, if you want?'

'I don't usually talk about it.'

His gaze dropped from her face to the floor. This was always the worst of it. Kids who felt ashamed of the fact that they were victims. Adults who kept on carrying the shame, unable to set it down. In Tom, it was somehow unbearable. She reached out to him, brushing her fingers against his jaw.

'Don't, please. It's...'

'I know.' His voice was harsh. 'It's nothing to be ashamed of, I've been told that. I'm nothing like my father. I've heard that one too.'

'Who told you?' She was hoping against all hope that this wasn't the first time that Tom had talked about this. That someone had been there for him.

'For the first year or so, after I left home and went

to medical school, it was as if I was suddenly free. And then...'

'It all came back and bit you?'

He nodded. 'I couldn't sleep, and when I did sleep I had night terrors. I felt such rage, and it scared me. So I went to a counsellor and talked it through. She suggested ways to control the anger and got me back on track.'

Maybe it would have been better if his counsellor had suggested ways for Tom to get the anger out of his system, not just control it, but Cori knew that now wasn't the time to mention that. 'Is that why you decided to go into paediatrics?'

He grinned suddenly. 'That's what my counsellor said. Apparently I'm saving my internal child.'

'Maybe. People's motives aren't always as clear-cut as that. I imagine there was some element of conscious choice about it.'

Tom nodded. 'I know it's what I'm best at, and where I can do the most good. That's more than enough for me. If it's a consequence of what happened when I was a kid, then it seems a little ironic.'

'Maybe you're just sticking two fingers up at your father? Turning what he did into something good?'

'I like that idea much better.' He leaned back in his seat, looking at her steadily. 'You know I've wanted to—'

He stopped talking suddenly, his thoughts obviously racing.

'You've wanted to what, Tom?'

'You were talking about making sense of things by painting.'

'Yes. That's one of my ways of dealing with the world.'

'I was trying to make sense of things. I'd decided to write a letter... I started on it late one evening when I was in the office, but it just didn't seem to say what I wanted it to. I thought I'd leave it and come back to it, and locked the pages in my drawer.'

Immediately the thought came to Cori. Rosie. But she shouldn't say anything, not yet. There had been enough rash accusations flying around already today. 'Are they... still there?'

'I don't know.' He took a sip of his tea, winced as the hot liquid touched his lip, and set the cup down into the saucer with a rattle. Tom seemed in no hurry to go and have a look.

'I'll go. Give me your keys and—' He shook his head abruptly.

'Thanks, but you don't need to. This is my problem.'

'No, it's the unit's problem. Someone is talking to a patient's parents, giving them information that's both confidential and traumatic.'

'I know, and I need to sort that out. But I don't want to drag you into this.'

When was he going to learn? He might be able to do it all by himself, but he didn't need to. 'Okay. There's something you need to know, Tom.'

His gaze didn't waver. 'I imagine there are lots of things I need to know.'

'Well, this one's important. Letting your friends help you isn't a sign of weakness.'

The bustle of the canteen no longer registered and all she could see was the anguish in his eyes. For long moments she held his gaze, hoping against hope that she could get through to him somehow.

'This one's for the door...only I guess you're not going to need that.' He'd pulled his keys from his pocket and was holding them up. 'This one's for the desk. Top drawer on the left. Right at the bottom there's an A4 envelope. It should be sealed.'

She took the keys. 'Thank you. I'll bring the envelope straight to you, if it's there.'

'Don't you want to know what's inside?'

'Of course I do. But I'm not going to invade your privacy to find out.'

He shook his head, a wry smile on his face. 'You're missing the point, Cori. The letter was addressed to you.'

Waiting for her wasn't as bad as he'd thought. Letting someone do something for him... It was a warm feeling, as if suddenly there was a place for him in the world. Tom tried to ignore the thought that maybe the important difference between this and all the other times that he'd turned away from anyone who'd got too close was that this time it was Cori.

He found that he had enough change to get another cup of tea, and this time he got a straw to drink it with. It must look a bit odd, but it meant that he could drink without getting the metallic taste of his own blood. Picking up a discarded paper from a neighbouring table, he turned to the crossword and tried to concentrate on the answers to the clues, instead of thinking about what Cori might be doing.

By the time she got back, he'd only got two of the easy ones. Sitting down opposite him, she drew a familiar manila envelope from her bag.

'I imagine this isn't how you left it.' She handed the envelope to him and Tom examined the flap. It had been carefully peeled open, and then stuck down again. He might not have even noticed if he hadn't taken the time to look.

'No, it isn't.' He laid the envelope down on the table. He could feel that there was more to come.

'Kate and the duty social worker have talked to the

Mortons. We know who did this.' She waited for his nod before she gave him the name. 'Rosie.'

'Yeah. I… That doesn't come as much of a surprise.' Everyone knew how much of a gossip Rosie was. He'd just never thought she'd take things this far.

'No. Not to me either. Apparently Mrs Morton came in to see Jamie yesterday evening, and she decided to go and have some tea afterwards. Rosie approached her in the canteen.'

'Rosie approached her?' Tom had been hoping against hope that this was somehow a mistake, something that someone had let slip. But it looked as if Rosie had gone out of her way to talk to Mrs Morton, and if she had, Tom couldn't protect her from a hospital disciplinary board.

'Yes. She told her about the concerns for Jamie, said that she thought we'd got it all wrong and why.'

'Why didn't Mrs Morton come back to the ward and ask what was going on?'

'Because Rosie made her promise not to. And, anyway, she wanted to talk with her husband first, and he works nights. So the first opportunity she got to discuss it was this morning.'

'So Rosie not only told her something enormously worrying about her own child, she also asked her to keep it a secret. That poor woman.' Tom shook his head. He supposed he wasn't really one to talk about keeping secrets. 'I imagine there's a fair amount of upset on the unit at the moment…'

'I didn't notice any.' She bit her lip. What the unit needed now was strong leadership, and Cori knew that as well as Tom did. He picked up the envelope, put it into his jacket pocket and stood up.

'Are you coming?'

She frowned at him, as if he'd just thrown her a mortal insult. 'What do you mean? Of course I'm coming.'

* * *

The unit had been sizzling with questions and uncertainties, and it seemed that Tom had the answer to all of them. He walked back into the unit and took charge straight away.

His first task was to talk to Mr and Mrs Morton, apologising to them both on behalf of the unit and shaking Mr Morton's hand. After some time spent alone with them, he emerged and made for his office, glancing at the staff assault report form that the social worker had left on his desk before screwing it up and throwing it in the bin.

Cori waited. Tom spoke to Kate for a while, and his body language was reassuring when concern shone from Kate's face. He joked with other members of staff and smiled at them, as far as his split lip would allow. Then he left Cori in the reception area and disappeared back into his office to speak with the hospital social worker. Just when it seemed that everyone was settling back into a normal Saturday lunchtime routine, Rosie walked through the doors of the unit.

This was *not* the neat, precise Rosie that Cori had got to know. Her coat was open and her scarf was dangling messily from her neck, while her face was streaked with tears and her hair scraped back into a messy ponytail. Cori moved in her direction to head her off, vaguely aware that Kate was doing the same, but Tom got there first.

Rosie gulped something about someone calling her, and that she needed to talk to him, and Tom hesitated for a moment. She gasped an agonised 'Please' and then he nodded, shepherding her towards his office, managing to give the impression of shielding her without actually touching her. Kate caught Cori's eye.

'He can't do that.' Kate knew as well as Cori did that in these circumstances it was a risk for Tom to go anywhere with Rosie on his own. She had no doubt that Tom would treat her kindly and with scrupulous professionalism, but with no witnesses, whatever was said or done it was Rosie's word against Tom's. And Rosie had already proved herself unreliable.

'I'm going after him.' Tom had waved both Kate and Cori away, but he was just going to have to live with her disagreeing with his judgement on this one.

Kate twisted her mouth. 'Good luck...'

She was walking so fast that she almost bumped into Tom, who was coming out of his office. She ignored him completely, craning around his bulk to see Rosie, sitting quietly now, being comforted by the hospital social worker.

Come to save me? He mouthed the words at her. His smile, lopsided because of the cut on his lip, made it clear that he liked the idea.

'No. I came to see whether I could get some tea for you.'

'That's a nice thought. Thank you.' He pulled the door closed behind him.

'Three cups and an ice pack?' They were alone in the corridor, and Cori risked brushing her fingers momentarily against his swelling jaw.

'Actually, just two cups, I don't think I can manage another one. The ice pack would be great, thank you.' His gaze caught hers, and heat sizzled between them. They'd come through this together. Tom, the man who needed no one and wanted no one, had accepted her help.

She turned quickly, before the touch turned into a kiss. 'Okay. I'll be back in a minute.'

They'd been closeted in Tom's office for almost an hour. Then Rosie had left with the social worker, and Tom had been ordered into one of the treatment rooms by Kate.

After that came the most tricky part of the morning.

'You're very rough. I hope you're not like this with the kids.' Tom shot Kate a rueful glare.

'She's not rough. If you'd just put that mirror down and stop trying to do it yourself, it would all go a lot quicker.' Cori grimaced at him.

Kate was shaking her head grimly. 'Doctors are always the worst.'

'Second only to nurses...' Tom's words were beginning to get a little slurred as the local anaesthetic took effect.

'I broke my finger. I don't think you fully appreciated just how much that hurt.'

'I seem to remember that you made it very clear at the time.'

Kate frowned at him. 'Are you going to stay still, or do you want me to call for restraints?'

'You keep your personal life out of this...'

The easy procedure of putting a couple of stitches in the cut on Tom's lip was performed with the maximum amount of fuss. Finally, Kate pronounced him likely to heal without a scar and Tom called a 'Thank you' to her retreating back.

'Are you ready to call it a day?' It suddenly seemed inconceivable to Cori that either of them should go anywhere without the other.

'More than ready.' He got to his feet and walked to the door, but instead of pulling it open he closed it. 'I've told Rosie to stay at home on Monday. I imagine that the HR department will be wanting to see her at some point, about speaking to Mrs Morton the way she did, but there's no need for her to be here.'

'That's thoughtful of you. You're not going to put in a complaint about her going through your personal stuff, are you?'

'No. She's in enough trouble already. I'm not going to make things any worse for her.'

'That's more than she deserves. It's difficult to imagine that she didn't know how much this might hurt you.'

'Maybe she did, and maybe she didn't. Maybe she thought that Mrs Morton would do as she asked, and keep what she said a secret.' Tom shrugged. 'In the end perhaps the secret itself is the most corrosive thing of all.'

He leaned back against the door, seeming suddenly tired. 'Come here.'

He'd always been so professional up until now, making sure he never touched her, never lingered in her gaze too long when they were at work. But this somehow felt right. As if now the different pieces of Tom's life, which he'd worked so hard to keep separate, were finally beginning to come together.

His arms were ready for her, and she felt a thrill of excitement when he folded them loosely around her shoulders. 'How do you feel now?'

'I want to kiss you. Although this isn't really the time *or* the place.'

'I won't tell if you don't…' Cori stretched up onto her toes, feeling his body react as hers moved against it, and kissed his cheek.

He hugged her tight. 'I'm… On second thoughts, I think I need a bit more time…'

'That's okay.' She moved away from him and he pulled her back.

'What I mean is that I can't kiss you right now because I have no feeling in my lips.'

'Ah. Well, you'll just have to let me do it for you, then.' Lightly, she kissed the very corner of his mouth, on the other side from the stitches. 'Can you feel that?'

'Yeah. Nice.'

'This?' She brushed her lips against his cheek, gently tracing the tip of her tongue around the curve of his ear, and heard Tom's sharp intake of breath.

He was luxuriating in her touch. Holding her close, as if that could chase away everything else that had happened today.

'Why don't you come with me to Ralph and Jean's this afternoon?'

He gave her a slightly sceptical look, which wasn't an outright no. 'You want to take me to meet your parents?'

'No, it's not like that. Ralph and Jean have open house on Saturday afternoons. Everyone drops in, they bring friends and friends of friends. It's like...'

'One big happy family?'

'You should try it.' The idea of finding comfort with your family had probably never occurred to Tom. Perhaps now was the time to show him what that was like.

They'd stopped off at Tom's house so he could change out of his blood-spattered shirt, and then at the supermarket to get a bottle of wine and some cheesecake, which Cori assured him would be exactly the right thing. He'd added a bunch of flowers for Jean to their basket, a bright arrangement of yellow and white blooms.

'I don't think I've ever met a girlfriend's mother before.' The large house was set back from the road and four cars blocked the driveway at the front so Cori swerved across the road to park.

'Well, there's no reason to start now. I'm not your girlfriend.'

That was actually wearing a little bit thin. They might not have had sex, but Tom didn't recall waking up in the middle of the night after an erotic dream about any of his other friends. Neither did he recall looking forward to

every moment he saw them, or finding that whole evenings had slipped away in their company and that he still
wanted to talk a little more.

'No. Well, that's a relief. How many brothers did you
say you had?'

'Four.' She turned to him, grinning. 'Don't tell me
you're afraid of my brothers.'

'Terrified. That's why you brought me here, wasn't it?'
Tom got out of her car, wondering if anyone would notice
if he walked around to open the driver's door for her, and
in a burst of courage he did it anyway.

'You look gorgeous.' He allowed his fingers to brush
against the soft fabric of her jacket, and she smiled up at
him, slipping her arm through his.

The lion's den wasn't as challenging as he'd thought it
might be. Ralph shook his hand and expressed concern
over the bruise that was rapidly forming on his face, and
Jean fussed over him, taking his arm and leading him
through to the kitchen, where a buffet lunch was laid out.

Adrian careened up to him, wanting to know whether
he'd treated any really gory cases recently, and was
shushed away by a woman who introduced herself as
Cori's sister. Then Adam, the brother who was a member of Cori's artists' group, found him and plied him with
questions about the unit, his enthusiasm just as great as
Cori's. All the while he could feel her gaze, and whenever
he was alone for a moment she was at his side.

'You like my family?' They were in the spacious conservatory, watching while everyone else traipsed outside
into the large back garden to inspect the summer house
that Ralph was building.

'They're like…' Tom had no point of reference for this.
'They're like a happy ending on TV. When everyone gath-

ers round the table for lunch together and the camera pans
out, leaving them to it.'

She chuckled. 'We have our ups and downs. Quite a lot
of them, actually.'

'A happy ending doesn't mean there won't be any ups
and downs. Just that you'll deal with them.' Tom surprised
himself with the insight. He'd always been more comfortable with the kind of happy ending that involved a fulfill-
ing career and resolute control over his personal life.

'Is that what you really think?' Cori clearly didn't quite
believe what she'd heard.

'Just trying the idea for size. And, yes, I really like
your family. Thank you for bringing me along with you.'

She smiled, flinging herself down into an armchair.
'They're the best thing that ever happened to me.'

'How old were you when you came here?'

'Seven. I'd been in and out of children's homes and fos-
ter-care before that. My father left my mother when I was
a baby and she started drinking. She'd get herself straight
and I'd go back to her, then she'd start drinking again and
everything would go pear-shaped.'

'Do you have any contact with her now?' Tom walked
away from the conservatory window, sitting down opposite her.

'No. When I was four years old she went on holiday
with her new boyfriend and left me with a neighbour.
When she didn't come back after two weeks, the neighbour called Social Services.'

'She never came back?'

'No. I found out later that Social Services had found
her but she'd refused to return. When I was twenty-one I
wanted to find out what had happened to her, and Ralph
helped me. She'd moved around a fair bit, got married for

a while and gone to live in Spain under another name. She died there. Liver failure.'

'I'm sorry.'

'It's okay. Actually, leaving me behind was the best thing she ever did for me. I couldn't believe it when I first came here. I used to get up ridiculously early in the morning and go downstairs and try to do the housework so that they'd keep me.' She grinned at him. 'I think Jean was afraid that if she taught me to cook, I'd be whipping up a Sunday roast at five in the morning.'

'So they taught you to paint instead. Sounds reasonable.'

'Actually, Adam taught me to paint. He's the same age as me but he was adopted at birth. So he got the job of making me feel at home when I arrived.'

'You're all adopted?' Tom was becoming fascinated by Cori's family. How it had been pieced together and yet seemed so solid.

'Yes, Ralph and Jean wanted kids but couldn't have any. Ralph had his own company, and had made a load of money through internet start-ups, and they decided they wanted to make a change. It was either this or go and drink cocktails on a beach somewhere. Ralph says that there are times when he wishes he'd chosen the cocktails.'

She turned as the door to the conservatory opened. 'There you are.' Jean smiled, flipping on the light, and Tom realised that it had begun to get dark while they were talking.

'I've been telling him the story of Ralph and Jean, and their incorrigible gang of kids.' Cori grinned up at her mother, and Jean laughed.

'I wouldn't say you were quite a gang. Are there any dirty plates in here?'

'Nope.' Cori got to her feet. 'You look tired, Mum. Sit down, and I'll do the washing-up.'

'That's all right. Grace and Adam are in there.'

'I'll go and help them, then. Sit down, will you?'

Jean nodded wearily. 'Yes, I think I will. Just for a minute.'

Tom went to stand and follow Cori into the kitchen, and Jean waved him back into his seat. 'You should be taking it easy too. That face looks painful.'

'It's not as bad as it looks. I want to thank you for your hospitality this afternoon. I imagine Cori told you that this morning's been difficult…'

'No. But I've seen enough split lips in my time to know that someone punched you.'

'Yeah. It was a misunderstanding. I'll have to work on doing things a little better next time.'

'Don't shoulder too much of the blame. A misunderstanding's never any excuse for violence.' Jean made the observation quietly.

In the last few moments Tom had just confided more, and received more back, than he'd ever shared with his own family. He felt suddenly thankful that Cori had found Ralph and Jean.

'I appreciate you saying that.'

Jean smiled, leaning back in the comfortable armchair. 'It's been a pleasure having you here. Cori's very excited about the project at the hospital. She says she's learning a lot.'

'Well, we've had our ups and downs.'

Jean looked at him thoughtfully. 'A learning experience for both of you, then.'

'It certainly is. Cori gives as good as she gets.'

'Always.' Jean smiled. Her eyelids were fluttering as if she was fighting off sleep. 'I'm…shlore…um…shlertain…'

'Jean?' Tom was suddenly alert. When Jean didn't respond to him, he rapped out her name. 'Jean!'

Her right arm fell from the arm of the chair. When Tom knelt down in front of her, he saw that her right eyelid was beginning to droop.

'Cori… Cori…' he called into the kitchen, as he pulled his phone from his pocket and dialled.

CHAPTER ELEVEN

'HE'S VERY GOOD-LOOKING.' Grace and Adam had been teasing Cori about Tom ever since she'd walked into the kitchen, and she was just about to let them do the washing-up by themselves.

'And he seems like a nice bloke.' Adam added to the ever growing list of Tom's accomplishments.

'Got a good job.' Grace chimed in with another one. 'What's his car like? It's got to be better than yours.'

'Why do cars matter? And, anyway, what's wrong with my car?'

'Not big enough, for a start. You need a van, like mine, to transport all your stuff.' Adam nodded sagely.

'Why do I need a van when you've got one?' Cori looked around as she heard Tom calling her from the conservatory.

Grace cupped her hand behind her ear, winking at Adam. 'Do I hear thy lover calling…?'

There was a note of urgency in his voice, which both Grace and Adam seemed to have missed. Cori dropped the plate she was soaping back into the sink, and hurried out to find Tom.

He was kneeling in front of Jean, his phone held between his shoulder and his ear. As she entered the conservatory she heard him say the word *stroke*.

'Mum…?' Tom beckoned her over and Cori saw that Jean's face was drooping downwards on one side.

'Your mother's having a stroke.' Tom spoke firmly, his voice low. 'I'm calling an ambulance now.'

'What do I do?'

'Hold her hand. Talk to her.' Someone spoke at the other end of the phone, and he turned his attention to them.

All she had to do was listen to Tom. *Don't think…don't question.* He knew what to do and he'd get Jean through this. Cori took her mother's hand between hers. 'It's okay, Mum. We're all here and Tom's calling an ambulance. It's going to be okay.'

She felt a tremor in her mother's grip that might have been some kind of reply and might not. Tom finished his call and slipped his phone back into his pocket.

'I'll stay here, and I want you to go and get your father.' His voice was quiet and measured, showing no sign of the stress of the situation. 'We're going to keep things quiet and comfortable for your mum. Do you understand?'

'Yes. Thanks.' Cori turned back to her mother. 'Mum, I'm going to get Dad. I'll be back with him in one minute, and in the meantime Tom's going to stay here with you.'

She didn't want to think about whether her mother understood, or what the convulsive jerk of her fingers meant. Laying her mother's hand back carefully into her lap, Cori ran through the kitchen, past Grace and Adam and into the garden. 'Dad… Dad…come quickly,' she called to Ralph, who turned, walking towards her over the grass.

'What's the matter?'

'It's Mum. She's had a stroke. Tom's with her.' She gripped Ralph's hand tightly. 'He's called an ambulance and we're waiting. Tom says we have to stay calm, and that we have to talk to her, reassure her…'

Ralph's face blanched, but he nodded. Wordlessly he

hurried into the house, walking straight past Adam and Grace, who were on their way out to see what was happening.

'Cori...?' Adam followed her inside, catching her arm.

She repeated the news. Each time she said it, it seemed a little less unreal. Grace started to cry and Adam nodded. 'I'll tell the others and we'll round Adrian up and keep him quiet. Go with Dad.' He wound his arm firmly around Grace's shoulders. 'All right, Gracie. We'll do this together.'

Cori stopped outside the door of the conservatory, and took a breath to calm herself. When she entered, Tom stood. 'Cori, I need you to help me. I'm going to move Jean onto the couch. Laying her down will help the blood flow to the brain.'

'Let me...' Her father was hanging on to her mother's hand.

'No, Dad. Let Tom do it, he knows how to lift her.'

'Yeah. Sorry.' Ralph pressed the palms of his hands to his temples, moving away from Jean.

'It's okay.' Tom was calm and reassuring. 'Just let us make her comfortable, and then you can be with her.'

He lifted Jean carefully, while Cori supported her head, laying her down gently on the sofa. Jean moaned, trying to speak, and Tom caught her flailing hand. 'You're doing really well, Jean. Just lie quietly and we'll get you to the hospital.'

Cori pulled up a chair for Ralph and he sat beside Jean, holding her hand and talking quietly to her. Tom straightened, his gaze fixed on the pale, suddenly frail figure lying on the sofa.

'How is she, Tom? Please tell me...' Cori whispered, dreading the answer.

'We've got to her quickly, and that's going to make a

real difference to how well your mother recovers. When she gets to the hospital they'll do a scan, and if it's an ischemic stroke…'

'What…?' Cori could feel tears welling in her eyes.

'If it's a blood clot, they can give her drugs for that.' She felt his hand on her arm. 'Hang in there. I can take care of what's needed medically, but it's up to you to keep things calm and quiet, and let her know that you love her.'

'Okay. Will you talk to Dad? Tell him what's going to happen next?'

He nodded, and Cori took her father's place, while Tom drew him to one side to talk to him. Somehow she found some words, and as she talked, she became more and more sure that her mother could hear her.

Her eyes filled with tears. When she'd heard Tom say *stroke*, all she'd been able to think about was an emergency, with blaring sirens and flashing lights. But he'd created a calm and peaceful atmosphere, one where Ralph had been able to hold Jean's hand and tell her how much she was loved. It was a precious gift.

She felt Tom's hand on her shoulder, and she bent and kissed her mother's fingers, then moved away so that Ralph could sit back down next to Jean.

When the ambulance crew arrived they seemed surprised by the lack of panic in the house. Then the paramedic saw Tom, and nodded to him. Tom spoke to her quickly and then the paramedic walked over to Jean, bending down so that she was in her line of vision.

'Hello, Jean, we've come to take you to hospital…'

Cori heaved a sigh of relief. The first and most dangerous part was over.

Tom and Ralph had gone with Jean in the ambulance, and Cori had followed with her brother Iain in his car, leaving the others at home with Adrian. There had been a scan, a huddle of doctors, comings and goings, and a transfer up to the stroke unit. Through the whole process Tom had been with Ralph, guiding him and keeping him strong. Finally, they were told they must leave for the evening, and Cori kissed her mother, leaving Ralph by her bedside to say goodbye.

Iain grasped Tom's hand in his usual vigorous hand-shake. 'Thank you for everything, Tom.'

'My pleasure.' Tom looked as drained as Cori felt, but he still had a smile left for Iain, even if it wasn't the most effusive she'd ever seen.

'I'll wait for Ralph and take him home. Do you guys want a lift anywhere?'

'That's okay. I'll walk Cori home.' Tom spoke for both of them. He seemed to know that the thing she wanted most was just to walk for a while in the cool air and clear her head.

'Right you are. Come for lunch, eh? Soon.' Iain's gaze included both Tom and Cori in the invitation and Cori's nod accepted for both of them.

They walked together out of the hospital, not a word passing between them, and not even the brush of his fingers against hers. But as soon as they were on the pavement Tom curled his arm around her shoulders in an expression of easy warmth.

'Your mum's in really good hands.'

'Yes, I know. Thank you.' Cori felt her lip begin to quiver. 'I told her that she was going to be okay…'

'You did the right thing.'

Cori heaved a sigh. 'I'm not going to ask whether I lied or not. I'm just going to believe that I didn't.'

He pulled her a little closer. 'That's a really good way of looking at it. However much we'd like to, no doctor can tell anyone with absolute certainty that they'll recover from something like this, but I'm as sure as I can be that Jean will. It'll take some time, and she'll need some help...'

Cori laughed. 'You've seen my family. She was there for us when we needed her, and we'll always be there for her.'

'And Adrian?' Tom had been obviously concerned for Adrian before they'd left for the hospital, making time to speak to him alone and reassure him.

'We'll all look after him until Ralph and Jean are back in action. Maybe it'll be a good thing for him in the long run, seeing her come back home and being involved a bit with her rehab.'

Tom nodded. 'He'll see that not everyone who goes to the hospital dies there.'

'Yeah.' There, a little thrill of pleasure to end a day that had held precious little to recommend it. Tom had been taking notice, the way he always did, and he'd remembered Adrian's fear of hospitals.

They reached her doorstep, and stopped. The last thing Cori wanted was to part from him now, after everything that had happened today, but she wasn't sure how to ask him inside.

'Are you tired?' He seemed to know the right question to ask.

'I should be. I'm not, though.'

'I feel the same.' He looked speculatively at his car, still parked outside in the road. 'You want to go for a drive?'

Perfect. The adrenaline in Cori's system was begging her to either fight or fly, but there was nowhere to go, and a feeling of obscure dread had been pooling in her stomach for the last hour. 'I'd love to.'

'Me too.'

They went inside to collect a flask of hot chocolate, which Cori insisted on making, even though Tom seemed to know a better recipe. She took her warm coat from the cupboard and found a dark green scarf that she hardly ever wore but which quite suited Tom when he wound it around his neck, tucking the ends into his leather jacket. And then they got into the car and just drove.

They passed through brightly lit main streets, filled with Saturday evening crowds, and quiet back streets. The road began to climb as they skirted around Hampstead Heath, houses and shops giving way to trees and park-land. Then Tom steered off the road and cut the engine.

'What a view!' Cori had driven past this spot before, where a gap in the treeline suddenly allowed a view right across London. In front of her the lights of the city were spread out like a twinkling carpet.

Tom got out of the car, opening her door and helping her out. Cori's limbs felt stiff after the hours of tension, and she almost stumbled into his arms. Almost but not quite. The last few inches were all of her own volition.

He settled against the side of the car, his arms clasped loosely around her, and she leaned against him, allow-ing his bulk to support her. 'I can see the London Eye...' She pointed to the right of the sparkling horizon. 'And the Shard.'

'Docklands and... What's that building? Over there?'

'I'm not sure. I don't recognise it; it must be something new. They keep building new landmarks.'

She felt his chest rise and fall against her shoulder. 'How are you doing?'

'I'm good. Thanks, Tom. If I'd gone home, I would have just cried on the sofa all night.'

'You can cry here if you like.' He bent down, his lips grazing her ear. 'It's a therapeutic exercise, and I wouldn't want to stop you.'

'No, I think I'm good.' She laid her head against his

chest, watching the lights, feeling the tension ebb out of her. 'Up here, I feel that everything's going to be all right.'

'It is. I know you're scared for your mum, but she's going to be okay.'

Something wistful in his tone made her want to ask, and the intimacy of this moment made it all right to do so. 'What about your mother? Is she…?'

'My mother died when I was twelve. Cancer.' His embrace seemed to tighten a little, as if he suddenly needed to hold on to her.

'I'm sorry. I shouldn't have asked.'

'If I hadn't wanted to answer, I would have said so.' He puffed out a breath. 'I have a lot of experience in not telling people things.'

'That's not very reassuring. I'd far rather you were a bit more…transparent.'

Tom chuckled quietly. 'You're not up for the discovery process, then?'

She turned in his arms, reaching up to clasp her fingers behind his neck. 'It might be a little frustrating at times, but on balance I'd say it's worth it.'

He folded her in what was unmistakeably an embrace. Not two friends clinging together for comfort, or huddling close in the cool air for warmth. 'There's so much I want to say…to explain to you. I tried to write it all down, but that didn't go so well. And now isn't the right time…'

'There's no such thing as the right time. And no such thing as a place to start.' She snuggled into his warmth. 'But if you ever find that you're in that wrong place and time…'

He took a deep breath, as if he was getting ready to hurl himself from a precipice. 'My mum always used to tell me not to get in his way, not to annoy him or make any noise. When he was in one of his moods, we'd both be walking on eggshells for days. When she died, I thought that maybe if I'd protected her a little better...'

'There's nothing you could have done, Tom.' She stretched up and kissed his cheek. 'You know that. You were a child, and it was up to the adults in your life to protect you. You are not responsible for your father's actions.'

He nodded. 'I know. Feels good to hear you say it, though.'

'Want me to say it again?'

'As many times as you like.' He kissed the top of her head. 'Are you getting cold?'

He'd had enough. She could feel it had been an enormous effort for him to say even that much. 'I wouldn't mind some of that hot chocolate. Can we stay here, though? Just for a little while longer?'

'As long as you like.' He let her go, brushing her hair back from her face with his fingers. 'You know, up here it almost feels that anything's possible.'

If only. Cori watched as he opened the car door, leaning inside to get the flask. If everything really were possible, then Tom would be able to see past everything that had happened to him. And if he did, he'd see that she was waiting for him.

CHAPTER TWELVE

CORI WOKE IN his arms. Not quite the way she might have hoped, but yesterday had been so extraordinary that pretty much anything went. Whatever got you through.

And last night, that had meant going back to Tom's house. He'd promised her a bed in the spare room for the night, and she'd taken him up on the offer because she hadn't wanted to be alone. And being with anyone other than Tom would have been alone. But in the quiet darkness her thoughts had begun to race, and even though she'd tried to go to sleep, she hadn't been able to. Tom must have heard her crying, because he'd been there, wrapping her in a quilt and carrying her through to his own bed.

They'd talked and he'd comforted her. And then they'd drifted off to sleep together. Now he was fast asleep, the morning light filtering through the curtains and bathing him in a warm glow. He looked like some kind of warrior angel, square jawed, his fair hair spiked around his head like a messy halo. One that had taken a little wear and tear lately, by the look of his lip and the corner of his mouth, which was now swollen and discoloured.

His eyelids flickered open, almost as if her gaze had actually warmed his skin. However battered and bruised he was, however slow and tired, he was still beautiful when he woke.

'Hey there…'

As he began to come to his hand drifted to his lip and Cori caught it, pulling it away. 'Don't touch.'

'No.' He wound his fingers around hers. 'How are you doing?'

'I'm fine.'

'Really?' Tom rolled on his back, holding her hand above his face. 'You're not just saying that?'

'No. Thanks for last night… What are you doing?' He was examining her hand carefully, spreading her fingers, running his thumbs over her palm.

'Just looking. You have very nice hands. Soft.'

'You don't have some kind of hand fetish, do you?'

'I don't think so.' Tom thought for a moment. 'What would you do if I told you I did?'

'I'm not sure. Show you the other one, maybe?'

He chuckled, twisting around and propping his chin on his hand, turning the full force of his melting blue eyes on her. 'What happens now, Cori?'

Good question. In fact it was the only question worth asking at the moment. She'd just woken up in his bed, with Tom lying beside her. True she was wrapped up in a T-shirt, sweatpants and about three layers of bedding, but those eyes of his were as naked as sin, and about fourteen times more tempting.

'I… I suppose the excuse about you being my boss is wearing a bit thin, isn't it?'

'Yeah. It's only for another three weeks and, anyway, I'm still waiting for you to actually do anything that I tell you to.'

'It could still cause difficulties. In the unit, I mean.'

'I'm very good at keeping secrets. You know that.' He flashed her a conspiratorial look.

'I…' She faltered. She could spend all morning in bed with Tom and no one would ever know. 'I'm not…'

He nodded. 'You're not looking for a fling. In particular, you're not looking for a fling with the hospital's most notorious philanderer.'

'That's not what I was about to say.'

'No, you'd probably put it more diplomatically. But the fact remains that I didn't leave home with a blueprint tucked in my pocket, telling me how a happy family might operate. And family means a great deal to you, I saw that yesterday.'

'Does that matter so much?'

'Yeah, I think it does.' He picked up her hand, pressing her fingers to his lips. 'I might not hold any records for the length of my relationships, but one thing I've never done is lie. The only time I've been happy in my life is when I've been alone, with only myself to answer to. I won't pretend that I'm in it for keeps when I'm not. Least of all with you, Cori.'

The temptation to tell him that temporary didn't matter, and that she'd take anything that he offered, was almost overwhelming. But that would sound a lot like begging for his attention. The thought made Cori feel suddenly cold, and she sat up quickly, taking a swathe of bedding with her.

'Don't kid yourself, Tom. You're not breaking my heart.'

He looked a little nonplussed. Maybe Tom didn't realise that his honesty had touched a nerve. That saying it out loud had suddenly made his inability to commit very real and impossible to ignore.

'That's good to know.' He spoke quietly, his gaze on her face.

She was an inch away from taking it all back and flinging herself into his arms, but the consequences of that were unthinkable. Other women might be able to handle temporary, and do it with a smile, but Cori couldn't. When it came to the crunch, the small child, in pain and longing for a family to call her own wasn't so very far from the surface.

'I'm sorry, Tom.' She reached for him and then thought better of it. 'I just think that… We were both upset last night and I'm so grateful that you were there for me. Let's just leave it at that.'

'Friends, you mean.' He rolled away from her, sitting on the far edge of the bed, his back towards her. *Friends* suddenly seemed an awkward and rather cold word, an excuse for not being able to be anything more.

'Yes. Friends would be good.'

He'd got out of bed, and left Cori to her own devices, while he went downstairs to make breakfast. Pausing by the mirror in the downstairs bathroom, he gave a little groan of disgust. No wonder she'd turned him down, when he was looking like this.

The look of reproach in his own eyes stopped him short. He might have got very used to covering up awkward facts with other people, but since when had he been unable to face the truth in the privacy of his own bathroom? The cut on his lip would heal, and she still wouldn't want him. That was set in stone, immutable.

She was right. They shouldn't kid themselves. He was the guy who didn't do for ever and he'd rashly thought that it might be okay to not do for ever with a woman who'd been hurt too much already. He should be ashamed.

'Friends, eh?' He quizzed his battered alter ego, staring at it hard in the mirror, wondering if it might come up with some much-needed advice. Tom couldn't imagine how just being friends with Cori would work out.

It was going to have to. There was nothing else. However much else he had dared to dream about, he had to put those thoughts aside, and deal with reality. Count himself lucky that he hadn't blown it entirely with her, and somehow remove the feeling, burned into his brain, that he never wanted to wake up again without her there.

It had been three weeks since Jean's stroke, and Adrian was sitting by her hospital bed, peeling the lid from a yoghurt carton. He carefully set the carton down in front of her and handed her a spoon. Cori watched as her mother slowly began to feed herself.

Tom had come to the house and explained everything to Adrian, telling him exactly what his mother needed and how he could help her. His confidence had been well founded. When Jean had recovered enough for Adrian to be allowed to visit her, they'd all seen another side to him. The boy who everyone reckoned had ants in his pants, and couldn't sit still for a minute, was gentle and patient with Jean, and the two were forming a very special bond.

'I think I've just about seen everything now,' Ralph observed, his voice quiet so as not to interrupt Jean's concentration.

Cori smiled up at her father. He was beginning to look less haggard, and she knew that he was sleeping better than he had. Eating better too if Iain and his wife had had anything to do with it.

'Don't eat too fast. You've got lots of time,' Adrian admonished Jean solemnly, waiting patiently while she slowly enunciated her reply.

'Do you want a break, Dad? I'll stay here.'

Ralph shook his head. 'No, thanks, love. I went down

to the canteen when Grace brought Adrian in after school. I'll take him home in half an hour.'

'Okay. I'll be here for a while, so I'll come up again later.'

'Working late again?' Ralph gave her a knowing look, which Cori ignored.

'Yes. When Tom finishes, which should be about half an hour from now, we're going to spend the evening building a tree.'

'Really?' Ralph raised one eyebrow, inviting her to continue. '*Building* a tree?'

'Yep. There's a playroom next to the art room, and we're building a model of a tree in there. It's a wishing tree. You know, people write things down and hang them on the tree...'

The idea of a wishing tree had come from Cori. She'd mentioned it to Tom, thinking that maybe a large branch or a picture of a tree on the wall would do the job perfectly, and then the whole thing had spiralled out of control.

'There's a wooden trunk and branches...' Cori indicated the curved shape with her hand. 'Maureen, one of the women who works here, her husband's a carpenter and he cut them from my sketches. They're going to be fixed to the wall, and the leaves will all be of different coloured fabrics.'

'I'll have to take a look at this when you've finished. Is this what you've been raising the money for?'

'No, it hasn't cost anything. I got three bags of fabric offcuts from my friend who works in a fashion house, and Tom got the wood from somewhere. It's nice wood too; I varnished a bit to try it out and it was a beautiful colour.'

'Sounds as if you two make a good team.' Ralph's eyes twinkled with humour and Cori frowned. That was exactly what she didn't want to hear. She and Tom *could* have made a great team, but that was just another missed opportunity now.

'Is that a problem?'

'No. But my placement is nearly up.'

'There isn't any rule which says you can't meet up with him after that, is there?'

No. But it wasn't going to happen. They'd made sure of that by pushing the boundaries too far. Ever since that morning, when they'd woken up together in Tom's bed, they'd been drifting apart. Their shared goals at work still drove them, but it was a journey full of awkward silences and feelings that would never be expressed.

Tom's appearance, at the other end of the ward, diverted Ralph from any more difficult questions.

'We were just talking about you.' Ralph shook Tom's hand warmly.

'Yeah?'

Cori felt herself flush, in response to the flicker of self-consciousness that had shown on Tom's face. 'I was just telling Ralph about the wishing tree.'

Ralph nodded. 'It's a nice idea. You seem to have achieved a great deal...'

Cori silenced Ralph with a glare before he could utter the forbidden word. *Together* wasn't something that she allowed herself to think about where Tom was concerned any more.

'I bumped into Jean's doctor on the way in.' Tom seemed just as eager to change the subject as she was. 'He said she's doing really well, and that she'll be going home soon.'

'Yes, we've been talking to Social Services and getting everything ready for her. We've got a way to go still, but we'll get there.' Ralph brightened a little at the thought.

'Absolutely.' Tom had always been positive, even in

those first uncertain days after Jean's stroke. Cori wondered how they would have managed without him, and dismissed the thought. She'd find out soon enough how well she would manage without him.

Ralph shook Tom's hand again, as if he couldn't reiterate that message of thanks enough, and Tom turned, walking to Jean's bedside. He produced a comic from his back pocket for Adrian, and took Jean's hand, facing her to catch her attention.

'How do you feel?'

Jean nodded. 'Good. Good.' Her speech was still slurred, and she tended to communicate in monosyllables still, but she was getting better every day.

'That's great. You're doing very well.' He backed the statement up with a smile, and Jean managed a lopsided effort in return.

Adrian's enthusiasm for the comic, and Jean's obvious wish for a hug, were managed faultlessly. Tom supervised the removal of Adrian's shoes, and lifted him carefully onto the bed next to Jean, spreading the comic out in front of them, and Adrian started to leaf through it slowly. After submitting to yet another of Ralph's handshakes, Tom shot a glance at Cori and she nodded. Their next stop was the wishing tree.

It had taken three evenings to finish the tree. Tom never tired of watching Cori work her magic. She had an uncanny knack of making something out of nothing. A few pieces of wood and some material were all she needed and she'd made something fabulous out of it. The curves of the branches seemed to beckon to him to touch them, and the carefully arranged colours of the leaves rippled through the tree like sunlight.

'Well...?' She stretched her arms, suppressed a yawn

and stood back to take a look. Tom could have kissed her there and then. If he'd thought for one moment that the accompanying wish would come true, he would have thrown caution to the wind and done it.

'It's wonderful. I love it.'

She nodded, surveying the tree thoughtfully. 'I think…' She selected another fabric leaf from the pile on the table and fixed it carefully, covering a square inch of blank wall. Then she moved another leaf a couple of inches to the left. Tom knew that she'd be stopping in front of the tree and making small alterations for a while before she would be completely satisfied.

'That's better.' She seemed content enough for the time being.

'Ready to make a wish?'

'Me?' Cori turned to him, shaking her head. 'No, not me. I don't want to go first.'

He should have known better than to even ask. During the last three weeks, their own wishes had been a no-go area.

'Maybe tomorrow.' Tomorrow was the last day of Cori's attachment to the unit. Maureen had been surreptitiously organising a small surprise party for her, and that would be an ideal time for everyone to share their wishes on the tree.

'Yes. That sounds like a good idea.' She was staring fixedly at the tree, as if looking at him was forbidden. Suddenly Tom wanted to share his wish with her now, not in front of a room full of people.

'Actually, I do have something.' Before he had time to change his mind Tom reached for one of the coloured tags that Cori had made.

'Do you?' She gave him a startled, wide-eyed look.

'Yeah.' He picked up a pen and wrote. 'Do you want to see?'

Cori eyed him suspiciously, but when he handed her the tag she took it and read what he'd written.

'Oh... Oh, that's really nice.

I wish that every child could grow up free from the fear of violence.

She tipped her shining face up towards him and Tom felt a little dizzy. They'd spent a lot of time together in the last three weeks, but determined activity had prevented them from daring to talk about anything that didn't pertain to their work. He suddenly realised how much he'd missed that.

'Are you sure you want to write your name?' She twisted her mouth in a wry smile. 'I think there might be one or two people on the unit who haven't heard the story of what Rosie told Mr Morton yet.'

'If there is anyone, send them to me and I'll fill them in on the details. It's been a secret for too long now, Cori. If I'm to be an advocate for children who are going through the same thing I went through, I need to be honest about what happened to me.'

'An advocate...' There was a telltale glint of a tear in her eye as she turned away from him. The thought that Cori still might be moved to tears for him made his heart lurch in a wild expression of forbidden joy.

Suddenly she was full of energy, bustling around, tidying up the mess they'd made while they worked. Hiding her tears from him. Tom tucked the wish into the pocket of his shirt. He'd hang it on the tree tomorrow, with all the others.

'I have one too.' She was still again, looking at him thoughtfully.

'What is it?'

'That I can keep up with you when we run on Sunday. And that we raise lots of money for the unit.'

'Whose idea was this?'

'I don't remember. Yours?' Tom turned his melting smile onto her.

'What was I thinking?'

He shrugged. 'I think it was rather a good idea.'

'I'm not so sure. I shouldn't have eaten all that cake on Friday. It was lovely of everyone to throw a party, but I'm regretting it now.' Her stomach felt as if it had a lead weight in it.

'The cake's not going to make any difference to you. You're just searching for something to be nervous about.'

'I don't want to mess up...'

Tom shook his head, obviously realising that he wasn't getting through. 'Just trust me, eh? I'll get you there.'

Despite her nerves, this felt like a turning point. They'd always enjoyed running together, and today the impending race seemed to have wrought a change in Tom. He seemed happier, less tense.

She felt his hand close momentarily around hers, giving it a squeeze. Smiling up at him, she took a deep breath. That was better.

The pairs of runners were working their way steadily through the streets of London, towards them. Through the City, which would be deserted on a Sunday morning, across London Bridge and then following the south side of the river until they reached the Jubilee Footbridge. Cori and Tom were second to last in the relay, running along the Embankment towards the Palace of Westminster.

The run was already a success. It had been talked about and re-posted from one social media account to another.

People had smiled when they'd seen the posters that Cori had designed, and the local paper was reporting on the run.

Donations had flooded in, and if the runners could complete the course first they stood to raise even more money. There would be enough for the project in the art room as well as much-needed equipment for the play room and the wards. What had started out as a fun run, had turned into a serious event.

'No pressure…' Cori didn't want to think about what they could do with that money. They weren't there yet.

'Nah. No pressure. Just keep up with me, and we'll make it.'

She rolled her eyes. Just keeping up was a lot more difficult than he made it sound. Numbly she followed everything that Tom did, warming up for the run, loosening her muscles, trying to keep her head clear of everything other than the oft-repeated mantra. They were going to make it. They were going to make it.

'Any minute now…' Tom seemed relaxed and ready to go. He stripped off his tracksuit bottoms and started to jog on the spot.

She could see the two runners coming towards them. There was no sign of the team travelling on the Underground yet. Helen Kowalski was running with her new fiancé and Cori stepped forward, ready to receive the baton.

She felt it slap into her hand, and her fingers closed automatically around it. She heard Helen shouting encouragement behind her, with what must have been the last of the oxygen in her lungs. Tom was off and running beside her, pacing her at exactly the speed he knew that she could match…

The pavement was wide, and this early on a Sunday morning it wasn't crowded. She felt good, strong, and she moved forward to run next to Tom. He flashed her a grin, checking the timer on his wrist.

'On schedule.' He didn't waste any words, but it was good to know. They'd started before the Underground team, but there was no way of knowing how much of a lead they had over them, or how long their opponents' journey would take. That element of uncertainty, which had helped to attract sponsors, was killing her now.

She fell into Tom's easy rhythm and forgot about everything else. Just the beat of their footsteps, the tempo of her breathing. One step at a time, each one bringing them nearer to their shared goal.

They ran together along the Embankment, Tom steering her around the people walking ahead of them. 'You're doing great. Just keep going.' He was well within his own capabilities and had breath to spare to encourage her.

Two-thirds of the way there she began to weaken. This was the crunch point, where she pushed through the tiredness and simply concentrated on keeping up with him. Her thoughts seemed to shimmer then crystallise on one thing. The smile he would give her when they made the finishing line together. It wasn't far away now and she concentrated on that.

'Cori…!' It was his urgent cry that told her she was falling. She heard rather than felt the sound of her knees hitting the pavement, and screamed in frustration.

'No…' She tried to get up but she'd lost control of her limbs. Ahead of her, only a hundred yards away, Gemma was waiting to take the baton, which seemed to be rolling away from her in slow motion.

'I'm okay. I'm okay.' She gasped the words, and made a grab for the baton. Somehow she managed to get hold of it and she pulled herself up onto her hands and knees. She was going to make it, even if she had to crawl.

Tom had stopped and was lifting her to her feet. She took a couple of tentative steps and then one leg gave way and he swung her up into his arms. 'All right. Just hang on…'

He started to run. Cori dug her fingers into his sweat-shirt, hanging on for dear life, trying to help him by supporting her own weight a little. She could hear his heart pounding, feel his breath, coming quick and hard.

'Yes-s-s…!' She heard a cheer from the group waiting by the station entrance, and felt Gemma snatch the baton from her hand. Tom stopped running, letting her feet slip to the ground but still holding her tightly against his chest. When he had caught his breath a little, he walked her the few steps to a couple of fold-up chairs that had been quickly vacated for them by the timekeepers.

He waved away the offers of help that came from the people around them. He wasn't the only doctor here—practically everyone had some kind of medical qualification—but he was the only doctor that Cori wanted and he seemed determined that he would be the only doctor she would have.

'Are you all right?' He was still breathing hard, but all his attention was on her.

'I'm okay.' She looked down at her knees and saw that blood was beginning to run down one leg.

'Sure? Let me look…'

'In a minute, Tom. I'm all right, just a skinned knee.' She felt her elbow begin to throb and peered at it. 'And elbow.'

'Did I hurt you when I picked you up…?'

'No, but you're annoying me now. Stop fussing and sit down will you?'

He opened his mouth, clearly intent on fussing a bit more, and then thought better of it. 'Fair enough. If I find out you're hiding anything, you're really in trouble.' Cori shot him a glare and he took the hint and sat down next to her.

Someone wrapped a blanket around her. A medical kit appeared out of nowhere, and Tom took charge of it.

'Blimey. You lot come prepared.' She surveyed the contents of the large box.

He shrugged. 'I suppose doctors and nurses know all the things that might happen.'

'What's that?'

'Nothing to concern you. You're obviously not in cardiac arrest...' He turned to see two figures hurrying out of the station and shot Cori that bright, melting smile that had carried her through the pain barrier. 'There they are...'

The team that had been travelling by public transport handed over their baton in a rather more civilised fashion than Cori had managed. All the same, she'd done it first, and that was what mattered. Commiserations were offered when they saw her knees, and someone fetched her a warm drink.

Kate arrived on a bicycle, bringing their things, and Cori slipped gratefully into her coat, while Tom put on his sweatpants. Kate tutted at the state of Cori's knees, and made a show of rolling her eyes when she saw that Tom was intent on dressing the wound.

'Good luck with that one. I'd have a nurse do it personally; we're much better at that kind of thing...' She laughed as Tom ostentatiously nudged her out of the way. She collected the next runners' things and got back onto her bike to take them on to the finishing post.

Cori waved her off as she set out along the cycle lane. Another cyclist, dressed in tight-fitting shorts and carrying a messenger bag, swerved across her path, making her wobble slightly, and she called a few indignant words after him as he pedalled away.

'Look, he nearly hit Kate…' Cori's indignation was shattered by a sudden, high-pitched scream, and she looked up to see a little girl of about five years old lying on the pavement and the cyclist riding away, without even looking back.

The child's mother was only two feet away, with a younger child in a pushchair, and she rushed to comfort her daughter, who flung herself into her arms, crying. Tom and a couple of the others were hurrying over to see if they could help, and Cori followed them, hobbling stiffly on her injured leg.

The woman seemed nonplussed at first, and then unable to believe her luck. Cori supposed it wasn't every day that you had two doctors and an ambulance driver on hand to help when your child took a nasty tumble. It seemed that, as Head of Paediatrics, Tom had pulled rank and was attending to the patient.

He helped the woman up, and delivered her child back into her arms. Someone wheeled the buggy behind them, and they all trailed across to the two fold-up chairs. Tom guided the woman into one, and Cori sat down in the other.

'What are you all doing here?' the little girl's mother asked.

Tom was working his charm and the little girl was responding shyly. Her mother obviously felt confident enough to let Tom get on with it.

'Oh, it's a charity run. For the hospital where we work. We're raising money to kit out an art room in the paediatric unit.'

'Good for you.' The woman smiled. 'I'm Lucy.'

'Cori.'

'I don't think that you're a *real* doctor...' The little girl's voice broke into the conversation, and Lucy flushed.

'Of course he is, Amy.'

Tom was laughing. 'She has a point.' He reached into the medical kit and pulled out a stethoscope, hanging it around his neck. 'There. Is that a bit better?'

Amy nodded, and Cori shrugged in Lucy's direction. Bringing a stethoscope to a fun run might be construed as over-packing, but she supposed it had come in useful.

'The man knocked me down.'

'I saw that, sweetheart. You took a bit of a tumble there. Can I look at your knee, please?'

Amy nodded, pulling at the large hole in her woollen tights. Her gaze wandered to Cori's leg and she craned around to look at it. 'Did you get knocked down?'

Cori laughed. 'No, I fell over. I was trying to run really fast and I tripped over my feet.'

'Ouch!' Lucy sympathised with her. 'You made the finishing line, though.'

'Yep. She made it.' Tom was smiling as he carefully swabbed Amy's knee.

'With a little help. Tom ended up carrying me for the last few yards.'

'Whatever works.' Lucy glanced at Tom, and then shot Cori a mischievous look. 'And it's all for a good cause.'

'Yes. One of the very best.' Cori let her gaze slip towards Tom. She never tired of watching him with his young patients. He had such a knack of getting children to trust him, making them smile. But, then, children had a habit of recognising a good heart when they found it.

'You've been very brave, Amy. Just one more thing to do, we're going to stick a plaster onto your knee.' Tom held up a large plaster and Amy nodded.

'Then Carly...?' Amy was having difficulty getting her tongue around Cori's name.

'Yep. Are you going to help? Since you know what to do now?'

'Yes-s-s!'

Amy supervised, while Tom swabbed and dressed Cori's knee, nodding her head in approval as he carefully taped a wad of gauze over the graze. 'You didn't say that Carly was brave,' Amy reproved him gently.

'That's right. Thanks for reminding me.' Tom turned his gaze on Cori, tenderness spilling from his eyes.

'You're very brave, Cori.'

He managed to say it all in just those few words. All the effort they'd put in, all the frustration and the pain. All the preparation and work it had taken to find sponsors. It had all been worth it for those simple words of praise from Tom.

CHAPTER THIRTEEN

SHE HADN'T SEEN Tom since the car that had taken them both home from the run had dropped her off outside her flat. Jean was out of hospital now, and Cori was staying with Ralph and Jean for the week to help them out.

Tom had never been far from her thoughts, though. In the evenings, when Jean and Ralph went to bed, Jean to rest and Ralph to read at her side, Cori painted. The canvas on which she had sketched his portrait, when she'd still believed that something between them had been possible, slowly took shape.

It seemed that he thought of her too. There were texts from him every day. Sometimes a question about the art-room project or about how Jean was doing, and sometimes just, How are you?

And on Friday evening came the text Cori seemed to have been holding her breath for the whole week.

See you tomorrow.

The tomorrow that Tom referred to was an early start. Even though Cori had told Tom that he didn't need to be there, and that the artists' group could begin work by themselves, he was waiting for her when she got to the hospital, all sleepy blue eyes and tousled hair. He helped unload the crates from the van, and when the other volunteers arrived he made tea for everyone, went to the canteen for egg-and-bacon sandwiches, and then made sure that he spoke to everyone, thanking them for being there.

The room had been cleared, and it was strictly off limits to patients and their families for today on account of the paint fumes. In amongst the bustle of activity they found themselves suddenly alone.

'Have you heard about Rosie yet?'

'Yes. They gave her an official warning and she's written a letter of apology to Mr and Mrs Morton. A secretarial post has come up in another department, away from the main hospital site, and she's decided to transfer over there.'

'It's probably for the best. After all the bad feeling in the department about what she did.' Cori couldn't bring herself to completely forgive Rosie for what she'd done to Tom, even though Tom himself had worked hard to smooth things over with the Mortons and had probably saved Rosie's job.

'We all need a second chance from time to time.' He stepped to one side to allow Adam to finish spreading a plastic sheet across the carpet. 'I'd better get out of your way.'

'Oh, no, you don't. There are some overalls in the crate over there.'

He raised a questioning eyebrow. 'You need a pair?'

'No. You might if you're going to help, though.'

He shook his head. 'I'm no artist.'

'Well, that's good, because I'm not looking for an artist.' Cori had already decided that she wasn't taking no for an answer.

'I suppose I should… Can't I just make the tea?'

'No. What's wrong with doing a little painting?' Cori found the drawing she'd made of the final design for a quiet area in the corner of the room, and looked for the appropriate bundle of stencils, which she'd packed last night, pulling them out of the box. Tom was eyeing them suspiciously.

'I need you to paint. We can't finish without you...' That wasn't exactly true. The project had been organised at short notice, and the seven artists who'd been able to make it here today would have to work hard, but they could do it. In truth, someone willing to make the tea and keep everyone fed would be a great deal more of an asset to the team than someone who needed to be taught how to use a stencil.

She took his arm, and felt the muscle swell under her fingers as if he was about to pull away. 'Tom, whoever took this away from you, it's time to take it back.'

'You don't *really* need me...' He was looking around at the bustle of activity in the room. 'It looks as if it would be better if I stayed out of the way.'

'That wouldn't be the point, Tom. What we're doing here is all about inclusivity, getting everyone involved, whoever they are. I won't leave you behind.'

He heaved a sigh. 'I suppose maintaining that I'm not in your patient group isn't going to work, then.'

'Not for a moment. None of this is about sorting people out into groups, it's about embracing what we all have in common.'

'Okay.' He held up his hands in a gesture of mock surrender. 'What do you want me to do?'

'This corner's yours. Here's the design and the stencils, and the paint and mixing trays are over there. Do you know how to use a stencil?'

'Nope.'

'Find some overalls, then, and I'll show you.'

All his life Tom had known that hanging on to his resolutions was the thing that made him strong. Whether they were big ones, like studying hard and getting out of his home, or the little ones, like never picking up a paintbrush again. And yet somehow Cori made him at least want to try to let go a little.

She showed him how the stencils worked together, building up layers of colour until the whole design was finished. How to fix the stencils to the wall, and how to sponge and brush on the paint. Apparently airbrushing was the next thing in her Pandora's box of treats, and she intended to show him how to do that after lunch.

He was left alone with a pile of stencils, paint, brushes, a blank wall, and a heart that was threatening to thump its way out of his chest. Why? It was just an old paintbox. Why did it matter so much?

'Come and see this.' Cori's voice broke into his reverie, and he realised that in half an hour he'd done nothing. She'd told him to look first and then paint, so he guessed he had an excuse.

'I thought you wanted me to paint.' He grinned at her, hoping the smile would soften the starkly empty wall that stood in front of him.

'You can take a break.' She ignored the fact that *taking a break* implied that he'd already done something, and beckoned for him to follow her.

As she walked along the corridor, heading for the ward reception area, she slipped her overalls from her shoulders, tying the sleeves around her waist. It was the way he'd first seen her. An old sweater, paint-spattered overalls, her hair tied up in a messy arrangement on the top of her head. This time she had marks around her eyes, the impressions from the goggles she'd been wearing to spray paint, and in an odd way that only added to the allure. Tom followed her with the same dogged joy with which he'd followed the trail of glitter from the car park.

There was a little huddle of people crowded around the nurses' station. As they approached, Maureen turned towards him.

'What are you doing here today?' Tom saw that there was a younger version of Maureen, obviously her daughter, standing next to her.

'What, and miss all the fun? We brought cake.'

'Home-made...' Cori was practically dancing on the spot with glee. 'Look, there's enough for everyone.'

'Maureen, you're a star. And you've brought... Amelia?' He searched for the name and found it.

'Milly...' Clearly the dark-haired teenager was of an age when her given name had become a burden and amendments were necessary.

'Sorry. Milly. It's great you came, thank you.'

'Milly was rather hoping she could paint...' Maureen leaned over towards him and Tom deflected the question with a look towards Cori.

'Yes, of course. I'm so glad you came. We have overalls and face masks to spare.' Cori beckoned towards Milly, who brightened immediately and followed her along the corridor without so much as a backward glance at her mother.

'She's growing up.' Tom remembered the shy child that Maureen had brought to work with her when he'd just been starting out in the unit. 'Bring your daughter to work day' had been a revelation to him when he'd first started work here. Seeing parents and kids who actually had conversations with each other.

'Yes, she is.' Maureen smiled after her daughter. 'She can be a bit stroppy at times, but she chose to come here today instead of going out with her friends.'

'She seems a great kid. I'll bet you're proud of her.' A lump began to form in Tom's throat. What was this? He

dealt with parents and their children every day. Why did
today suddenly seem so different?

'Yeah, I'm proud. In between the times I feel as if I
could murder her...' Maureen turned as Cori and Milly
reappeared at Tom's elbow.

'We've got an idea...' Milly's eyes were shining.

Cori turned to Tom. 'We thought we could open the
blinds in the glazed wall, between our room and the next
one, so that anyone who wanted to come and watch could
do so, without getting any of the fumes from the paint.'

'Sounds good to me.'

'And *then* we thought...' Milly chimed in.

'Yes. Then we thought that we could make it a bit like
a peep show. You know, at the seaside.' She frowned. 'I'll
sketch it out so you can see what I mean.'

'Just do it. As long as it's safe, it doesn't damage anything, and you don't get in the way of the work of the
unit, go for it.' They'd talked and planned for long enough.
Today was a day for doing.

'Okay.' Cori exchanged a private nod of excitement with
Milly. 'Let's go, then. There are some bits and pieces in
the van that I need some help with...'

He'd intercepted Cori and Milly manoeuvring a large piece
of art board through the entrance doors, and had managed to guide them through to the art room without flat-
tening anyone. He'd helped Maureen carry the boxes of
cake through to the kitchen, and had then spent some time
with Kate, checking on one of the patients who was giving
her cause for concern. And the blank wall was still there,
waiting for him.

When he got back to the art room, he found that Cori
and Milly had almost finished their project. The art board
had been laid out on the floor, cut to shape and painted.

The quick, expansive brush strokes took away nothing from the design—it was a seaside Punch and Judy stall, with a red and white striped canvas, a couple of seagulls perched on the top and a cloudless blue sky behind it.

Cori took a moment to stand back and look at their work, and gave a little nod. 'That's great, Milly. Really nice. It'll be dry in half an hour and we can put it up outside.'

'What's next?' Milly was beaming.

'Why don't you go and see Adam? He'll show you how to help him with the spray paint. Only put your mask on.' She watched as Milly bounced over to Adam and then she turned to Tom. 'How are you getting on?'

'Still in the thinking stage.'

She nodded. 'Right. Well, that's good. Any clue about when you'll be ready to move on? Bearing in mind that we need to finish sometime before midnight.'

He grinned. 'We have that long?'

'Well, I'd prefer it was a bit sooner. But however long it takes.' She looked up at him, and suddenly he knew. Somewhere in the vibrant warmth of her eyes he found his safe place.

'You want to know something crazy?'

'Yeah, go on. Crazy always turns me on.' She was moving with him slowly away from the others into a quiet corner of the room.

'When I was eight years old my grandparents bought me a painting box. I loved that box, and I kept it under my bed, where no one could get at it. One day I spilled some paint on the carpet. I managed to clean it up mostly but…' Tom shrugged. The words had suddenly become too much for him.

'Your father took them away?'

'He smashed the box and threw it away with the paints.

I told myself that I didn't like painting anyway, and that I didn't care. He couldn't touch me.'

'That's not crazy, is it?'

'The crazy part is that I haven't picked up a paintbrush since.'

'So...you want to share my paintbox?' She shot an impish look in his direction.

'I would...' Suddenly everything seemed so simple. So easy. 'Actually, I would love that.'

'Right. Let's get started, then.'

CHAPTER FOURTEEN

His wall had become *their* wall. As Tom worked, stencilling the designs, he began to realise that Cori had more in mind than a simple mural of intertwining leaves and flowers. The lush vegetation that he was painting was just a backdrop for animals and birds, painted separately, ready to be mounted onto the wall to give a three-dimensional effect.

'Very neat. What are they painted on?' He watched as she laid the creatures out on the floor.

'Plastic. It's durable and light. I'll fix them on with these spacer pegs behind them so they'll stand away from the wall and give a bit of texture.' She looked up at him. 'That's the theory anyway. It's a bit of an experiment, and I'll be wanting you to report back to me on how it performs in practice.'

'You're going somewhere?' He was concentrating on dabbing paint onto every part of the wall exposed by the stencil, and the question just slipped out before he'd had a chance to think about it.

She gave him a puzzled look. 'I don't work here any more, remember?' She gestured him back to work.

He carefully peeled the stencil off the wall, admired his handiwork and consulted Cori's sketch to see what he had to do next.

'You don't *have* to stick to the plan.' She was looking over his shoulder. 'Actually, a few more leaves here…'

She waved her hand vaguely in the direction of the design on the wall, and Tom laughed. 'I've only just got to grips with how to do this. Now you want me to start making it up as I go along?'

'All right. Since you're not quite ready to break free and follow the tide, perhaps you'll let me add a few freehand bits.'

'Good idea.' Cori would always be happiest with one toe slightly outside the boundaries. Working freehand and dealing with life as it came along. And Tom was happy to watch that for the time being.

Even though the room wasn't quite finished, it looked stunning. The kids who had gathered outside to enjoy the peep show had banged on the window in delight, and the artists working on the designs had made faces back at them. They drank tea and ate cake as they worked, continuing through lunchtime and finishing early. At four o' clock it was decided they could do no more until today's paint was fully dry, and Tom extended an invitation to everyone to meet at the local pub.

'You shouldn't have done that.' Cori was curled up in her seat like a cat, warm and with a full stomach. 'We usually have a whip-around to pay for food and drink.'

'It's the least I could do. Did you see the kids' faces?'

'Yeah. Makes it worthwhile.' She stretched languidly and settled back in her seat, smiling lazily at him. In that moment the whole of the evening and the possibilities of the night to come seemed to open up before Tom.

He could wait, though. While the artists tipped their glasses to empty them and put them down on the table, reaching for coats and scarves. While Milly, who had been allowed to come with them on the express condition that she only drank orange juice, waved goodbye and was watched to her mother's car outside. While the landlord collected the plates and glasses, leaving an empty table in front of them.

'Guess we'd better go. Unless you want another drink?'

'No. Thanks, but I think I'd like to lie flat on my sofa for about an hour.'

'Sounds good. You could lie flat on *my* sofa if you wanted. I have chocolate.'

She leaned towards him, the colour of her eyes seeming suddenly brighter. 'Are you trying to tempt me?'

He'd spent too long without her. And now it felt as if his world was shining with a brilliance that only Cori could create. He could no longer deny that he wanted to be with her tonight.

Tom smiled at her. That thousand-volt, X-rated smile, which she couldn't resist. 'I could leave the chocolate on your doorstep if that's a better idea.'

It probably was. But she didn't want today to end. Not here. Not now.

'You can't leave chocolate on doorsteps. It could rain and then it would get wet. Or the foxes might find it.'

'And that would be a sin.'

It was too late to weigh that one small sin against all the others that saving the chocolate might lay them open to. Especially as tonight they didn't seem so very sinful after all.

'So, what kind of chocolate do you have?'

'Truffles. Dusted with cocoa powder.'

She could almost feel them on her tongue. 'You keep a stock of them, do you?'

'No. I saw them the other day and thought of you.'

Satisfaction blossomed in her heart. 'So you've been planning this for a while?'

'There's no plan. That's the whole point, isn't it? There's nothing we have to do, and nothing we can't do.'

Her heart thumped in her chest. Cori could practically feel her cheeks flushing, her pupils dilating. All the little things that would tell him that *nothing we can't do* sounded just fine with her.

'Chocolate…may be a bad idea. Is there such a thing as a serotonin overdose?'

He grinned. 'Not unless you're taking medication that affects your serotonin levels. Got a headache?'

'No.'

'Feeling confused?'

'Not in the slightest.'

'I think you can stand a little more, then.' He leaned forward, and Cori shivered as his breath brushed her ear. 'Maybe a lot more.'

Warmth shimmied down her spine. 'And what about you? Can you stand a lot more?'

'I don't know. This isn't something I've done before.'

If that was his way of telling her that she was different from all the rest… Cori looked into his eyes, and suddenly it seemed that it might be.

'Then you'll be wanting me to lead the way?'

'Always, Cori. You get to call the shots.'

It took a man as strong as Tom to say that. To put what he wanted out there, and let her either accept or reject him. And she accepted him, just as he was. Wordlessly she stood, winding her scarf around her neck and pulling on her old leather jacket.

She clearly didn't quite believe him. Tom didn't totally believe it himself, but the feeling persisted. Cori really was different. He really hadn't been here before.

The car radio came on when he turned the key in the ignition and she turned the volume down a little but left the music on. They made the twenty-minute drive to his house almost in silence, and she followed him quietly to his front door. He slid the key into the lock and let her in, closing the door behind them.

He could see her silhouette and hear her breathing in the dark hallway. Smell the paint on her clothes and the light, musky scent of her skin.

'Cori, I…' He reached for her and felt her finger across his lips.

'It's okay, Tom. We don't need to talk about this.'

He curled his fingers around hers. There was every need to talk about it, however cold it seemed to say the words right now. They couldn't simply assume that they understood each other. 'Cori, I don't have any promises to give you. Tonight is the only thing I have.'

The last time they'd had this conversation she'd rejected him, and Tom wouldn't blame her if she did so now. But somehow he knew that she wouldn't.

'I know.' Her voice was quiet in the darkness. 'Tonight's enough.'

'You're sure?'

'You'll give me everything. Just for tonight?'

That he could promise. 'Yes, sweetheart.'

'It's enough, then.'

He wanted to tell her how special she was, but words could no longer compete with the dialogue of feeling that spun between them. Slowly, he backed her against the wall, hearing her sharp intake of breath as his body closed on hers. When he kissed her, she whimpered quietly.

Each one of his senses was raging, wanting her so badly that it hurt. He heard his own breathing quicken, along with hers, and buried his face in her neck. She wrapped her arms around his neck and he lifted her slightly, just enough that they were face to face, and felt her legs wind around his hips.

'I want to take you here. Right here, right now.' He whispered the words into her ear, and felt her body move against his. If she did that again, that was exactly what he was going to have to do.

'Yes… I want that too…'

'But then I wouldn't have the pleasure of soaping you clean. Wondering all the while what it feels like to be inside you.'

'Can we…?'

'We can do whatever we like…'

'To me? Will you do whatever you like to me?'

Her words broke him. Something inside snapped and then re-formed, wanting only to give Cori whatever she wished for. 'Whenever you want me to, honey.'

He'd kissed her in the darkness of the hallway until she could no longer disguise the fact that her whole body was crying out for him. Every time he touched her, heat seemed to bloom across her skin. Each time his body moved against hers, she felt her breathing quicken, her heart beat a little faster, in a spiral of longing that only he could satisfy. And Tom clearly had no intention of doing that just yet.

Finally he took her upstairs, stopping on the landing to kiss her again, before leading her into the bedroom. The heavy, cast-iron bedstead dominated the room, almost beckoning her towards it. A soft glow emanated from two table lamps, and Tom was showing no inclination to switch them off.

Cori had been banking on darkness and it taking him

only seconds to undress her. It looked as if she was going to be wrong on both counts. 'I thought that I might…' She pulled at a loose thread on her old sweater. 'I thought I might do this alone.'

He looked genuinely crestfallen. 'If you want.'

'I didn't exactly have this in mind when I dressed this morning.' She leaned towards him, nipping his ear. 'I've got my passion-killers on and—'

'Passion-killers, eh? You think they're going to work?'

He didn't wait for an answer but pushed her back onto the bed, leaning over her, kissing her mouth. As he did so, Cori could feel him unbuttoning her cardigan. 'I want to undo every button. I want to work out a way of getting you out of those overalls and see every inch of you as I do it.'

He made it sound like a good thing that she was wearing her oldest clothes. 'Yeah. I'm good with that.'

He rolled over, propping himself up on the pillows and pulling her astride his hips. Sliding her cardigan from her shoulders, he set to work on her shirt. When he had that unbuttoned he slid his hand under the T-shirt underneath and found the hooks at the back of her bra. One hand on the back of her waist steadied her and the other found her breast, teasing until she cried out.

'Now, please…'

'No, not yet. There's so much more…' He rolled her over onto her back and the sharp insistence of the moment subsided into a warm haze of wanting. She wriggled luxuriantly under him, and he chuckled.

'I'll get you back, Tom Riley.' She pulled at the front of his shirt and felt his weight on top of her, pinning her down. When she moved against him, he groaned.

'Cori…'

'Yeah.' Her hand slid between them, finding the zipper of his jeans. Two could play at this game.

* * *

They played at this game for as long as they could bear it. When they'd got each other out of their clothes he took her into the black, white and chrome bathroom, and they soaped each other clean. Then he wrapped her in a towel and carried her back to the bedroom, laying her down on the bed.

He was gorgeous, his smooth, tawny skin rippling over a strong, muscular frame. His eyes were the deepest shade of blue and his hair golden, standing up in spikes from where she'd dragged her fingers through it.

He took care of everything—pillows at her back, condoms ready for when they needed them. And now they were both trembling, unable to wait any longer.

She felt his hips nudging her legs apart. His fingers wound around hers. For one moment he was still, gazing into her eyes, and then she felt him slide slowly inside.

'Beautiful… Cori, you are so beautiful…' He wound one arm around her back, the other cradling her face in a gesture of shattering tenderness. They made love, staring into each other's eyes, dragging out each moment until she felt the orgasm begin to roll inside her. When he felt it too he thrust hard, sending her over the edge into a bright cascade of feeling.

He could barely hang on before the orgasm overwhelmed him. Taking him and dashing him against the furthest frontiers of what he thought his body was capable of. He knew that he called out her name, and that he was holding her close, but beyond that Tom was just a helpless mess of sensation, broken for the first time, and in love before he even saw it coming.

When he woke in the night he found her there, ready

to hold him and take him back inside her. She made him trust himself, believe that he could be the man he wanted. The man she wanted.

They slept and made love pretty much in equal measure until late in the morning. Got up slowly, showering and eating breakfast sprawled on the bed. Easing themselves into the day.

'You're going to work this afternoon?'

'Yes. I thought I'd take you home to change your clothes then we could go to the hospital together.' It wasn't Tom's usual modus operandi to spend the day with someone after sleeping with them the night before. People had things to do, and a modern relationship didn't require that two people cling together like limpets. But the idea of employing anything as premeditated as a modus operandi with Cori was downright ridiculous.

She grinned at him. 'I'll be needing new underwear.'

Tom tried to nod gravely, but could feel the corners of his mouth twitching. 'Another pair of passion-killers?'

Her brow wrinkled in thought. 'Well, you can only really get away with passion-killers if no one knows you're wearing them.'

'Something else, then?'

Cori's cheeks flushed pink. After what they'd done last night it seemed slightly incongruous that a discussion about what underwear she was going to wear should make her blush, but she somehow managed to carry it off. 'I...don't know.'

'So I guess that watching you work and imagining your perfect behind is going to take some improvisation?'

She leaned forward, running her finger along his jaw. And then, suddenly his whole world came crashing down.

'I love you, Thomas Riley.'

* * *

Rewind. Do something. Pretend your body was just taken over by aliens, and it wasn't you who said it. Panic seized Cori.

For a moment she thought that maybe it was going to be all right. That he'd laugh and tell her that he loved her too. But Tom would have to be taken over by aliens before he said such a thing.

'Cori, I…' He shook his head. 'We made an agreement.'

And he'd held to his part of the bargain. She should stick to hers, do them both a favour, and let him off the hook.

She squeezed her eyes shut, feeling tears well up against her lids. However embarrassing it was, she couldn't pretend that she hadn't meant what she'd said. Not after what they'd shared last night. Not even to save whatever was left of their relationship.

Moments ticked away before she heard his voice, calm and quiet. 'Cori, I've never asked a woman back to my place before.'

She opened her eyes. 'Say that again. While I'm looking at you.'

He met her gaze without blinking. 'I haven't asked a woman back to my place before. It's a thing I have.'

'What sort of thing?'

'My own space has always been very important to me. It *is* very important to me.'

'What are you saying, Tom?'

'I'm saying that you're special to me, and that you always will be. But I don't do love. I never have done.'

Something cold crawled across her heart, and then pride came to her rescue. 'Let's not pretend, eh? This was never anything other than a one-night stand.'

He said nothing. Cori could see she'd hurt him, but knew he wouldn't hit back at her. She should go now, before she opened her big mouth again and made things even worse. She stood up, and somehow her legs managed to support her weight. 'I think it's time you took me home.'

When he dropped her back at her flat Cori made it clear to him that she intended to work alone today. She showered again and changed her clothes, and then walked to the hospital. It took the whole of the afternoon to finish the murals in the art room and she worked steadily, no tears, no scene. When she was done she packed up her paints and walked out of the hospital, without saying a word to anyone. She was done. Finished. In every sense of the word.

She'd said he loved him. It wasn't so much the words that had horrified him, but the look in her eyes when she'd said them. Cori had really meant it. And in that moment he'd realised that everything he'd felt the night before was real. He loved her too.

She'd put her heart in his hands, and he was so afraid of dropping it. Letting her down, finding that he really couldn't change and give her all the things that she deserved.

So he'd told her the truth. He didn't do love. He didn't know how to plan a future together, or dream of having a family. And it wasn't fair to Cori for him to do all this for the first time, make every mistake in the book, and break her heart in the process.

His father had always made everything about what *he*'d wanted. *His* moods, *his* temper had ruled their household. Tom had promised himself that he would never be like that, and this was the ultimate test. He had to put aside what he wanted. He wanted Cori but he had to forget that and concentrate on what he was able to give.

And that was a heart that equated strength with being alone. One that had been taught to shy away from the

vulnerability of being in love. His father may have poi-
soned Tom's own dreams, but he would never allow him
to touch Cori's.

Tom opened the wardrobe in his bedroom, sliding out
the precious canvas and unwrapping it. Cori's painting,
the one that he had bought from the tea shop. At the time
his motive for buying it had been to give the fundraising a helping hand, but now it meant a great deal more to
him. The loneliness, so movingly portrayed, was something that she had learned to leave behind. But it was ir-
revocably his now.

CHAPTER FIFTEEN

WHEN THE LETTER from the hospital arrived, Cori had stared at it for a long time before opening it. Inside was a reference from Tom.

She stared at the paper, wondering if Tom really was responsible for this. It was his signature at the bottom, but maybe Maureen had written it and just pushed it in from of him to sign.

Trembling, she read the reference, word for word.

To whom it may concern...

It started off impersonally enough. Who she was, how long she'd worked at the hospital and in what capacity. Then...*then...*

Cori is not bound by convention in her approach to problem-solving...

Cori's breath caught, tangling in the memory that he'd said that once before to her.

Her solutions are both elegant and appropriate.

A tear rolled down Cori's cheek. It was as if Tom were standing in front of her, saying all these things.

*The artwork that she has left with us at the hospital
is enjoyed by everyone and is increasingly becoming the focus of a new culture within the unit—one
that encourages expression in a safe environment.*

*What is less tangible, but no less obvious, is the
touch of magic that all her artwork contains.*

It had to be Tom. He'd written that. Cori turned the
page to the end of the letter and stared at his signature.
He'd signed it. Put his name to it and sent it out so that she
could show anyone she liked what he thought.

She went back to the beginning of the letter, reading it
carefully, every word. Tom had covered all the bases, and
he had nothing but praise for her. Then the final paragraph.

*Cori was a great asset to the unit while she was here,
and I am convinced that she will go on to do more
good work. I am only sorry that budget constraints
mean that she will be doing that work elsewhere.*

She put the letter down on the counter top, breathless
with emotion, tears streaming down her face. There was
no way out, she couldn't pretend now that Tom didn't respect her. There was no doubt that he'd written this, and
no doubt that he was sincere, even if this was the last evidence of their parting.

She should text him, say thank-you. Perhaps add that
there were no hard feelings, but after the generosity of the
reference he'd written, that seemed grudging. Telling him
that it meant the world to her was out, as well. It did, but it
wasn't going to change things between them. He couldn't
love her. And so she couldn't bear to be around him.

Cori decided to think it over. She put the reference away
carefully in the drawer containing her passport, the state-

ments of the savings account that Ralph and Jean had set up for her, and the two battered baby photographs that she had of herself. All the things that meant something to her and which had shaped her life.

A long shower didn't make things any clearer, and neither did breakfast or an hour sitting in front of her easel without being able to even lift her paintbrush. She took a walk, got some shopping and carried it home. She still didn't know what to say to him.

The truth. If you don't know what to say, just say the truth. She picked up her phone.

Thank you. I regret nothing and wish you only happiness.

Cori stared at the words. It was exactly what she wanted to say to Tom, but it was incomplete.

Goodbye.

The word was stark enough, but it was the truth. Cori pressed 'send' before she could change her mind.

Almost immediately her phone signalled that he'd answered. Cori dismissed the idea that it was unlike Tom to be so attentive to his phone and that he must have been watching for a message.

I wish you all the things I couldn't give. Most of all magic.

Then the tears came. Not the half-hearted, sliding-down-your-face tears but great, gasping, runny-nosed sobs. It was really over. How could Tom ever know that the last word he would ever say to her would hurt so much? Because losing him had taken every last shred of magic from her life.

* * *

Even a life without magic had to go on. Cori threw herself into applying for jobs, attending one interview after
another. And her weekends were taken up with the artists' group, whose paintings were in such demand that
they had a waiting list.

'Wait, Milly, I'll take you home.' The group had finished another assignment and were packing up to go home.

'That's okay. It's only a fifteen-minute walk.'

It was dark, and Cori had promised Maureen that Milly
wouldn't come home on her own. The teenager had seemed
to grow up very suddenly since she'd started working with
the group at weekends, but she was still only fifteen and
Cori was still responsible for her.

'I thought you might give me a hand carrying these
boxes into my flat. Then I'll drop you home.'

'Okay.' Milly was surveying the finished wall painting
and the subterfuge was accepted. 'What do you think?'

'I think you did really well. The stencilling you did in
the corner there is lovely.'

Millie glowed with pleasure. 'I painted the little silver
swirly bits on later.'

'I saw. They make all the difference.' Milly was beginning to show real promise, and her painting was im-
proving as the artists in the group showed her tricks and
techniques. It was more than that, though. Milly's art had
a touch of exuberance about it. That indefinable magic
that Cori had seen draining out of her own work recently,
leaving it pale and lifeless.

'So you're pleased with the wall, then?'

'I…' The director of the centre had expressed her delight, and everyone else seemed satisfied. But there was
something missing, and Cori wasn't sure what it was.

'I don't know. I'm going to think it over and come back next week.'

'Finishing touches?' Cori nodded in reply. 'Can I come?'

'If you like. As long as—'

'My homework's done and my mum's happy,' Milly interrupted. 'I know.'

'Yeah. Sorry about that. But you have to take care of the practical side of things first.' It seemed to Cori that the practical side of things was all there was these days. The magic had packed its bags and gone on holiday, and her joy in her art was gone. She surveyed the painting thoughtfully. Maybe that was what the matter with it was.

Milly saw it first. Perhaps because she still lived in a world where fairies existed. 'What's this?'

There was a feeble glow coming from outside the big bay window in Cori's living room. When she walked closer to the glass, she could see that it was coming from the end of a wand, and that the fairy who held that wand had a familiar look about her.

Cori didn't need to touch the twists of wire and gauze outside, she knew exactly what this was. The fairy that she'd left on the bonnet of Tom's car had a tiny golden heart twisted inside its chest, which she'd put there to wish it luck in catching Tom's eye. And now she was suspended outside her own window.

'Cori…?' Milly was staring at her. 'You look really weird. You're not going to faint, are you?'

'No.' Cori grabbed at her easel to steady herself.

'Are you sure? I could call Mum…'

'No…no, I'm fine, really.' A trail of glitter led from the window to the small table on the paving stones outside. It snaked up the legs of the table and swirled around a circular box covered in gold paper and with a brown-and-gold bow on top.

'That's so pretty…' Milly had her face pressed to the glass. 'Did Dr Riley leave that for you?'

'What? How do you know that?'

'I don't. I don't know why I said that.' The guilty look on Milly's face said that she knew exactly why she'd said it. 'Mum'll kill me…'

Tom felt so close at this moment that Cori could swear she could almost touch him. She had to know. 'Look, I won't breathe a word, not to anyone, I promise. Did your mum say anything about Dr Riley?'

Milly hesitated.

'Please, Milly. Is he all right?'

'Mum said that he seemed really sad when you left. She says that it's a shame it didn't work out between you and him, and that she reckons he's working too hard. You won't tell anyone I told you, will you? Mum said we shouldn't interfere.'

'No, of course not. I won't tell a soul, I promise.' Maureen was probably right. It was better to leave things as they were. She would get over it eventually, and Tom would too.

She opened the French doors and looked out, half hoping to see Tom out there somewhere. It would get this over with quickly; she could remind him that there was no future for them and send him on his way. But the golden box and its fairy guardian were alone, so Cori collected them both up and brought them inside, putting them down next to each other on the coffee table.

'What are you going to do?' Milly sat down next to her on the sofa. Apparently they were in this together, and there was no question of Milly being dispatched home to allow Cori some time to think.

'I'm going to open the box.'

'Yeah. Good thought.' Milly nodded earnestly, as if they were making a decision on the right answer in a game show. 'See what's inside.'

Cori took the box on her knees and untied the ribbon. It occurred to her a little too late that it might contain something that Milly probably shouldn't see, but she dismissed the idea. Tom had more style than that.

'Oo-ooh!' The lid came off the box, and both of them sighed together.

'It's beautiful.' Milly whispered the words. Inside the box chocolate truffles were piled on golden tissue paper. 'What's that?'

'I think...' Cori twisted the box so that the tiny flecks on the chocolates caught the light. 'Yes—it's little pieces of gold leaf.'

'Really!' Milly's hand flew to her mouth. 'Real gold? Can you eat it?'

'Yes, it doesn't do you any harm.' Cori laughed. She could almost feel Milly's wonder cutting into the dead feeling that had surrounded her heart in the last weeks. 'Shall we try one?'

Despite Milly's impatience, Cori found a little cut-glass dish at the back of her kitchen cupboard and put two of the chocolates in it. Then she lit a candle and dimmed the overhead lights so that the gold decoration on the chocolate sparkled. This was just the way that Tom would have done it.

'Mmm. These are so good.' Milly licked her fingers to get the last taste of chocolate. 'Are you going to call him?'

Cori supposed that this was the reaction that she was supposed to have. But the chocolate was just lovely chocolate, not the delightful rush to the head that it seemed to be for Milly. And she wasn't going to call Tom.

'Maybe.' She couldn't quite bring herself to disillusion Milly. 'After I've taken you home.'

Milly had made a dash for her coat and made it absolutely clear that Cori was not invited in for a cup of tea on this occasion. Clearly she presumed that calling Tom would be at the top of Cori's list when she got back home and didn't want to keep her from doing that.

But chocolates and fairies didn't mean anything. They were evidence of Tom's charm, not that he'd changed. People didn't change, just like that, overnight, however much they wanted something. Cori had spent enough time waiting for her mother to change, to come back to her, to know that was a foolish dream.

She stared at the golden box sitting in front of her on the coffee table. It seemed to be mocking her now, daring her to think about everything that she'd lost. If she'd had any sense she would have given the chocolates to Milly so they weren't there to torture her, but somehow Cori hadn't been able to.

She shook her head at her own stupidity and reached to put the top back onto the box. Then she saw it. Nestled amongst the tissue paper, a ribbon with a tag on it threaded through the fob of a key.

'Tom… What have you done now?' The whispered words got no answer and Cori drew the key out of the box and read the words written on the tag.

Yours. Always.

It was an impossible dream. Tom's door key in her hand. The most precious thing he had was his own space, and now she had the key to it. Cori stared at the tag. What was hers? The key? Tom? It didn't say, and this was far too important for her to jump to conclusions.

It wouldn't work between them, they'd already tried once and failed. Cori repeated all the arguments to herself again and again, even as she was pulling on her coat and getting into her car.

A light shone from the downstairs front room of Tom's house. He must still be up. Perhaps he was waiting for her to call him or knock on the door. Well, she was going to call his bluff and use the key. When she did that, he'd realise what a crazy gesture all of this was and leave her alone.

She slid the key into the lock and it turned easily. There was no chain on the door and the deadlock was disengaged. Stepping inside, Cori felt her stomach lurch.

The noise from the heels of her boots was deadened on the thick carpet. When she pushed open the door to the lounge she saw Tom fast asleep on the sofa, a book upturned on the floor next to him where it had obviously tumbled from his hand.

She could wake him or… No, she wouldn't wake him. Just seeing him here asleep was chipping away at her resolve at an alarming rate. Quietly Cori picked the book up from the floor and put it on the coffee table, resting the precious key on top of it. Somehow she managed to turn and walk away.

'Don't…'

She froze.

'Not another step, Cori.'

'Or what?' She didn't turn to face him. 'What will you do, Tom?'

Cori was trembling. She knew that he wouldn't do anything to stop her from leaving, and when she did so she was going to be alone again. This had been *such* a bad idea.

She heard him move and he appeared in front of her, all tousled fair hair and bedroom eyes. Leaning back against the door, he pushed it shut, folding his arms. 'I'm not going to let you go.'

'You can't keep me here.'

For a moment they were at an impasse, each trying to stare the other down. Cori was the first to break. 'Tom, this is crazy.'

'You came.'

'I just wanted to call your bluff. To see you back down.'

He shook his head, the trace of a smile playing at one side of his lips. Did he really have to make it this hard? 'Not going to happen.'

'Okay.' She marched over to the coffee table, picked up the key and dangled it in front of his nose. 'Do you know what this means? *Really* know?'

'I know.'

Yeah, right. There was no trace of nerves behind the smile that was moving across his face. Not even the slightest hint that he had any idea just how much something like this would turn both their lives upside down.

'I don't think you do, Tom. It means that you don't have your own space any more. It means I can come and go as I please. No more control, no more keeping everything under wraps.'

His chest heaved as he took a deep breath and suddenly Cori saw all the doubt, all the fear. 'Yeah. It scares the hell out of me, but nothing scares me as much as losing you again.'

She turned away from him so he couldn't see her tears. 'Why do you have to make this so difficult?'

'Cori…' He almost choked out her name. He was close, very close, she could feel him behind her. 'If you tell me to let you go, I will.'

'Wha—?' She whirled around, and suddenly she was in his arms.

'If you tell me to leave you alone then I will. But you can't tell me to stop loving you. And you'll never stop me from wanting you in my life. All over my personal space, challenging me every day, making me angry…'

'Really?'

'Yes, and loving it better. I want you to know that I mean this. I know how afraid you are that I'll let you down but I'm asking you to put that aside and give us another chance.'

She could hear his heart beating fast against hers. Feel his arms trembling around her. 'Let me go, Tom.'

Almost immediately he stepped back. Then he turned away, a cry of harsh anguish escaping his lips as he stalked over to the fireplace, slamming his fisted hand down on the mantelpiece. She could see his back heaving just from the effort that it seemed to take to keep breathing.

'You have to believe me, Cori.'

'Why? You don't do love, Tom. You said it yourself.'

He turned, his face softening when his gaze met hers. 'Don't you see? You have to believe me. I gave you up. I wanted you so much, but I let you go so that I couldn't break your heart. And then I realised. If I can love you enough to give you up, then I can love you enough to make you happy.'

'That's…' It was either complete and utter madness or the most wonderful thing she'd ever heard.

'Yeah, crazy. I know. But that's how it is.'

'You left me because you loved me?'

'I left you because your happiness is more important to me than anything.'

'You idiot!'

'If you mean that I'm an idiot for letting you go...' He shrugged. 'Guilty as charged.'

Suddenly she knew. From the tips of her fingers right down to her toes she knew.

'You want me to take the key? Then make me.' Cori reached out her hand, tracing her fingers across his jaw. As soon as she touched him, happiness washed over her like a great wave.

One lone tear fell from the corner of his eye. Just one, but it was the beginning of everything, her whole future. When Tom reached for her, her legs gave way suddenly and Cori wrapped her arms around his neck.

'Sweetheart...' He lifted her up, swift and sudden, laying her on the sofa and pinning her down with his weight.

He unzipped her jacket and undid the buttons of the sweater underneath. Then her shirt, and Cori felt his hand slide across her skin. She wriggled underneath him. 'Upstairs...'

'Oh, no. You just made the rules, Cori. And you are going to beg me for that key before I take you upstairs.'

Cori lay naked on his bed in the morning sunshine. Last night had changed everything. It had shaken him to the core that she could give herself to him with such passion, and when she'd finally taken the key he had wept. Unashamedly, for the first time in his life.

Tom traced her spine with his finger, wondering if she thought any less of him for it now that the heat of last night had dissipated. She gave a little purr of lazy pleasure and rolled onto her front and Tom kissed the small of her back, working slowly upwards.

'That's nice.' She shivered when he got to her shoulder blades and he used one of his thumbs to work out a knot in her spine. 'Will you be there to wake me up tomorrow?'

'Are you in any doubt of that?' He found a growing area of tension between her shoulder blades, which told him that maybe she was, and dipped to brush a kiss there. 'I wouldn't have left that box for you if I didn't intend to be there for all your tomorrows.'

'What would you have done if I hadn't found the key? If I'd dumped the chocolates in the bin?'

'You would have put chocolate truffles into the bin? I don't believe it.' He chuckled, the laugh an expression of pure happiness, nothing more and nothing less. There was no need any more to use a smile to defend himself from the world.

'Would you have tried again? Sent something else?'

'Every day. Until you listened to me.' He kissed her shoulder, nuzzling against her ear. 'You, my love, would have been the target of a concerted and determined charm offensive. Only without the charm, since it appears you're immune to that.'

'Hmm.' She propped herself up on her elbows, gazing into his face. 'I'm almost sorry I missed it.'

'Well, I'm not letting up. I have a very pressing need to keep you exactly where you are.'

'I can't wait.' She leaned over and brushed a kiss to his lips. 'What's the matter?'

He couldn't hide even the smallest thing from her, the most fleeting of qualms. And he didn't want to. 'I wonder if you think less of me. I'm not the guy who has it all under control any more. Maybe I never was that strong.'

'Only the strongest man I know could translate what you went through when you were a child into the kind of care you give the kids on the unit. Only the bravest could bring himself to weep the way you did last night.'

Tom pulled her close. 'You know, I think I might just be home.'

'Yeah. Me too.'

CHAPTER SIXTEEN

THE TWO MEN standing in front of the painting didn't see the couple in the corner of the gallery. If they had, they might not have recognised the artist of the work they were currently considering, but they probably would have recognised the subject.

'It's…so lovingly done.' The older man looked thoughtfully at the picture. 'And yet there's a kind of sadness there. Do we know the artist?'

The younger man flipped through his catalogue. 'Ah, here. Corinne Evans.'

'I haven't heard of her. But this is very good. It has… life. Spirit.'

'Do you think it's a contender?'

'Definitely. I'll be watching Ms Evans.'

The men moved on to the next painting, this time shaking their heads. 'They prefer yours,' Tom whispered to Cori.

'Did you hear what he said? Luther Galloway said that I was a contender.' She clutched at his sleeve.

'And apparently you're someone to watch.' Tom planted a kiss below her ear, making her shiver. 'But, then, I knew that all along.'

'I'm so glad you entered it. I wouldn't have had the guts.' The painting usually hung in the hallway of their

home, but Tom had removed it and brought it here, entering it for the Galloway Prize on Cori's behalf.

He put his arm around her. 'There are a lot of really
good paintings here. But I know which one *I* like the best.'

Cori snuggled into him. 'You're biased.'

'Of course I am. I'm allowed to be biased in favour of
my soon-to-be wife.'

The engagement ring still felt a little odd on her finger,
and she had to look at it every now and then just to remind
herself why she felt like laughing out loud all the time. A
diamond, mounted on a platinum band and flanked by two
amethysts, which he'd claimed were the colour of her eyes,
it reminded her that this was all true and not just a dream.

'We should celebrate. Now that I'm no longer just the
acting head of paediatrics, courtesy of Dr Shah's early re-
tirement, and you're a contender for the Galloway Prize
and have a great new job.' He leaned over to whisper in her
ear. 'I was thinking that warrants a bottle of champagne
and a large bowl of strawberries. In bed…'

'I love the way you think. But I should give the champagne a miss.'

'Why?'

'I didn't get a chance to tell you, when you rushed me
out of the house this morning…'

'Sorry about that. I wanted this to be a surprise and
I was hoping you wouldn't notice that the painting was
gone from the hallway again. The excuse about refram-
ing it wasn't going to work a second time…'

He stopped short, as understanding dawned in his eyes.
'You're…giving the champagne a miss?'

'For a while. But I'll be eating for two, so I'm relying
on you to do some serious cooking. You might even have
to give me some lessons.'

He ignored the small group of people that had just

walked into the room and took her in his arms, kissing her. 'What do you say we bring our wedding date forward a bit? I want to be married to you when our baby is born.'

'That sounds wonderful. I love you so much.'

'I love you too.'

They sat together for a long time, watching the comings and goings in the gallery, happy just to be together. Cori gazed up at her painting of Tom.

'You know, I've suddenly realised something.'

'Yes? What's that?'

'I'm going to have to paint you again. I don't recognise that man.'

He looked at the painting, studying it thoughtfully. 'You mean the sadness.'

'Yes. You look so…haunted. And my sadness is there too.'

'That's not us any more, Cori.'

'No.'

He took her hand, leading her away from the painting and out into the sunshine.

* * * * *

MILLS & BOON®
Hardback – February 2016

ROMANCE

Leonetti's Housekeeper Bride	Lynne Graham
The Surprise De Angelis Baby	Cathy Williams
Castelli's Virgin Widow	Caitlin Crews
The Consequence He Must Claim	Dani Collins
Helios Crowns His Mistress	Michelle Smart
Illicit Night with the Greek	Susanna Carr
The Sheikh's Pregnant Prisoner	Tara Pammi
A Deal Sealed by Passion	Louise Fuller
Saved by the CEO	Barbara Wallace
Pregnant with a Royal Baby!	Susan Meier
A Deal to Mend Their Marriage	Michelle Douglas
Swept into the Rich Man's World	Katrina Cudmore
His Shock Valentine's Proposal	Amy Ruttan
Craving Her Ex-Army Doc	Amy Ruttan
The Man She Could Never Forget	Meredith Webber
The Nurse Who Stole His Heart	Alison Roberts
Her Holiday Miracle	Joanna Neil
Discovering Dr Riley	Annie Claydon
His Forever Family	Sarah M. Anderson
How to Sleep with the Boss	Janice Maynard

MILLS & BOON®
Large Print – February 2016

ROMANCE

Claimed for Makarov's Baby	Sharon Kendrick
An Heir Fit for a King	Abby Green
The Wedding Night Debt	Cathy Williams
Seducing His Enemy's Daughter	Annie West
Reunited for the Billionaire's Legacy	Jennifer Hayward
Hidden in the Sheikh's Harem	Michelle Conder
Resisting the Sicilian Playboy	Amanda Cinelli
Soldier, Hero...Husband?	Cara Colter
Falling for Mr December	Kate Hardy
The Baby Who Saved Christmas	Alison Roberts
A Proposal Worth Millions	Sophie Pembroke

HISTORICAL

Christian Seaton: Duke of Danger	Carole Mortimer
The Soldier's Rebel Lover	Marguerite Kaye
Return of Scandal's Son	Janice Preston
The Forgotten Daughter	Lauri Robinson
No Conventional Miss	Eleanor Webster

MEDICAL

Hot Doc from Her Past	Tina Beckett
Surgeons, Rivals...Lovers	Amalie Berlin
Best Friend to Perfect Bride	Jennifer Taylor
Resisting Her Rebel Doc	Joanna Neil
A Baby to Bind Them	Susanne Hampton
Doctor...to Duchess?	Annie O'Neil

MILLS & BOON®
Hardback – March 2016

ROMANCE

The Italian's Ruthless Seduction	Miranda Lee
Awakened by Her Desert Captor	Abby Green
A Forbidden Temptation	Anne Mather
A Vow to Secure His Legacy	Annie West
Carrying the King's Pride	Jennifer Hayward
Bound to the Tuscan Billionaire	Susan Stephens
Required to Wear the Tycoon's Ring	Maggie Cox
The Secret That Shocked De Santis	Natalie Anderson
The Greek's Ready-Made Wife	Jennifer Faye
Crown Prince's Chosen Bride	Kandy Shepherd
Billionaire, Boss...Bridegroom?	Kate Hardy
Married for their Miracle Baby	Soraya Lane
The Socialite's Secret	Carol Marinelli
London's Most Eligible Doctor	Annie O'Neil
Saving Maddie's Baby	Marion Lennox
A Sheikh to Capture Her Heart	Meredith Webber
Breaking All Their Rules	Sue MacKay
One Life-Changing Night	Louisa Heaton
The CEO's Unexpected Child	Andrea Laurence
Snowbound with the Boss	Maureen Child

MILLS & BOON®
Large Print – March 2016

ROMANCE

A Christmas Vow of Seduction	Maisey Yates
Brazilian's Nine Months' Notice	Susan Stephens
The Sheikh's Christmas Conquest	Sharon Kendrick
Shackled to the Sheikh	Trish Morey
Unwrapping the Castelli Secret	Caitlin Crews
A Marriage Fit for a Sinner	Maya Blake
Larenzo's Christmas Baby	Kate Hewitt
His Lost-and-Found Bride	Scarlet Wilson
Housekeeper Under the Mistletoe	Cara Colter
Gift-Wrapped in Her Wedding Dress	Kandy Shepherd
The Prince's Christmas Vow	Jennifer Faye

HISTORICAL

His Housekeeper's Christmas Wish	Louise Allen
Temptation of a Governess	Sarah Mallory
The Demure Miss Manning	Amanda McCabe
Enticing Benedict Cole	Eliza Redgold
In the King's Service	Margaret Moore

MEDICAL

Falling at the Surgeon's Feet	Lucy Ryder
One Night in New York	Amy Ruttan
Daredevil, Doctor...Husband?	Alison Roberts
The Doctor She'd Never Forget	Annie Claydon
Reunited...in Paris!	Sue MacKay
French Fling to Forever	Karin Baine